THE MYTHS OF TIME

THE MYTHS OF TIME

Twilight Tales
by
DAVID McGOWAN

SUNDIAL SUPERNATURAL

THE MYTHS OF TIME

First published by SUNDIAL SUPERNATURAL, 2017
An imprint of The Sundial Press

THE SUNDIAL PRESS
Sundial House, The Sheeplands, Sherborne, Dorset DT9 4BS
www.sundialpress.co.uk

A CIP catalogue record for this book is available from the British Library

Typesetting and Cover Design: Frank Kibblewhite

ISBN 978-1-908274-60-1
Printed in Great Britain
by 4Edge Limited

CONTENTS

THE TEST OF TIME

I

'FRANKLY I can think of no greater horror than the Christian concept of eternal life,' said Ormerod, spearing a roast potato with his fork. 'Stuck up there with a crowd of harping cherubs? No thanks!'

'But surely the idea of being reunited with loved ones on the other side is a reassuring one,' I replied.

'Loved ones?' my companion snorted.

'Your father, mother – and didn't you have a brother who passed on?'

'Passed on? Passed on indeed! Died! My brother died, Hopkins. Let's have none of this passed on nonsense. And as for being reunited with them: my father beat me mercilessly as a child, my mother died from cirrhosis of the liver – owing to the usual cause – and my late brother once attempted to drown me in the bathtub due to his insane jealousy. I can assure you I have no wish to clap eyes on any of them ever again, either in this life or another.'

'So you view life as being essentially without meaning?'

'Completely pointless, old man – chaos in action.'

'As a Christian I'm afraid I can't agree with you.'

'And as an atheist I can no more agree with your belief in a supernatural deity, or a child born without intercourse, given that it was pre-IVF, who could bring the dead, himself included, back to life.'

'These are trying times to be a believer,' I sighed. 'I suppose that's what having faith means.'

'What? The complete suspension of all logic?'

We each sipped our wine.

'Perhaps in time all will become clear,' I remarked.

'That's the first sensible statement you've made all evening, Hopkins – though for all the wrong reasons,' Ormerod replied.

'Then you believe we will get to the bottom of things in time?'

'I believe time is the bottom of things,' said my friend. 'It is the very heart of all things. The man who understands time will understand everything.'

'I don't quite follow you.'

'Tell me,' he said, 'what is time?'

His question left me flummoxed. 'Why, it's the – the continual moving forward – of events,' I finally managed triumphantly.

'Poppycock!' he replied.

'Then what is your own definition?' I asked, taken aback by his abruptness.

'I have none,' he said simply.

'Surely we can at least agree that time moves forward?'

'Sadly no,' he responded.

'But why not?'

'Because I have serious reservations regarding its very existence.'

'You doubt time exists?' said I, bewildered by the turn our conversation had taken.

'I do,' he answered, sawing at his well-done steak.

'But how can it fail to exist? We walked here using time – my watch hand is moving forward –'

'Your watch hand?' he burst out with a guffaw. 'What has that to do with time – save to show it as a man-made concept?' He leaned across the table, his voice becoming more animated. 'What is this present we inhabit, Hopkins? When does it become the past and what is its link to the future? I tell you the present no more exists than your Yahweh. It is impossible to pinpoint it – forever on the brink of the past and the future.'

'Then you at least believe in past times and future times?' I ventured.

'No,' he replied, refilling his glass. 'I cannot find it in me to believe in either.'

'Then what of history?'

'What of it?' he countered nonchalantly.

I shook my head incredulously. 'And yet you say that time is at the bottom of things?'

'I do.'

'It all seems to be a riddle with you,' I said, exasperated.

'It is, Hopkins,' he replied. 'It is – but one that I hope to solve some day.'

'In the future?' I replied, with my tongue firmly in my cheek.

'Touché my friend,' he laughed good-naturedly, clinking his glass to mine.

II

My meetings with Gerald Ormerod are few and far between. He is an intensely private individual – indeed I don't believe I ever heard him speak of any friends he had. He lives a solitary life in a small hamlet on the outskirts of Cambridge where I have no doubt he is as much of an enigma to his neighbours as he is to me.

I made his acquaintance in a very singular manner when I was walking down a narrow country lane near his home. He crashed into me while riding his bicycle round a blind corner. Bruised and battered as I was, he led me to his door and attended to my superficial wounds while apologies fled from his lips.

I say I am his friend, but in truth our relationship is more akin to dog and master – with myself as the canine.

He's best described as an eccentric character. A tall, gangly, thin-faced man with a tangle of shoulder-length black hair – always impeccably dressed in his favourite Harris tweed. A fascination with colour is another of his foibles. His shirt and tie will be yellow and red, blue and silver or violet and orange. He is not a man one passes by without noting.

The science of numbers has long held him in thrall. I believe he is one of the greatest mathematicians of this – or any other – century, despite having never attended university or taken a degree of any kind. His education is all of his own making and he is truly in command of a mind of which it can be said the mould was broken after his birth – a one-off, unique in every way.

Ormerod had a contempt for all modern conveniences. Neither landline nor mobile phone; computer or television set; DVD or CD player were to be found in his possession. That was what made it all the more surprising when my own landline rang early one morning and I answered it to find him on the other end.

'Hopkins? Hello old man.'

'Ormerod? Is that you?' I said, very much startled.

'Indeed it is – my apologies if I've disturbed you.'

'Not at all. Have you had a telephone installed at last?'

'No, I'm calling from a public phone box.'

'Is something wrong?'

'No – no … the thing is …'

'Yes?' I said as he hesitated.

'… I was wondering if you could possibly pop down to see me.'

'In Cambridge?' I asked.

'No – at my home.'

I'd known him over twenty years, but I would as soon have expected an audience with the Pope as an invite to Ormerod's home.

'Is everything alright?' I reiterated.

'Certainly – things are fine … at the moment,' he tagged on apprehensively.

'When would suit you?' I asked, by now actively concerned.

'I'm in your hands Hopkins – but asap if you can.'

'I could be there this evening.'

The note of relief in his voice was palpable. 'That would be excellent, Hopkins. Thank you. Take a taxi from the station – you know the address.'

'Yes,' I replied.

'Till tonight then,' he ended – and the line went dead.

III

Having arrived that night my first impression when my friend answered the door was one of shock, as he had shaved his head completely.

'All in the cause of knowledge, Hopkins,' he said, seeing my reaction.

He had become gaunt since our last meeting. His pale blue eyes seemed to hang listlessly in their sockets and he had developed the curious habit of clicking his teeth together in what I could only assume was some kind of nervous reaction.

As he showed me to my room I was amazed at how colourful the entire house was. Walls were painted vivid reds, blues and yellows. The furniture was also multi-coloured, ornaments too. It was as if a rainbow had crashed through the roof into his home.

Having dined on roast beef and potatoes – all of Ormerod's own making I might add, as he was the sole occupant – he led me to his study and gestured for me to take a seat in one of a pair of red leather armchairs. After pouring us both a generous whisky he sat down in the other chair and gave a thin smile.

'Cheers,' he said, raising his glass.

'Cheers,' I replied as my eyes wandered to the shelves of the book-lined room where volumes by Euclid, Pythagoras and Newton sat side by side with Einstein, Reeman and Gauss. *The Principia Mathematica* of Newton, in a cracked black and red leather binding, seemed to be particularly old.

'You're wondering how I manage to pay for all this?' said Ormerod.

'I presumed you had found the pot of gold at the end of your rainbow-coloured home.'

'It was much easier than that,' he replied. 'No spadework was required. There was a point in my life where I actually did hold down a job,' he went on. 'Given my natural ability with figures the Stock Exchange held out a considerable appeal to me in my youth and, as things transpired, I chose an excellent time to be there – just as the big bang began in the mid 80s. I invested any money that came my way in new technology shares and at the end of five years I sold up and found myself to be a very wealthy young man. My good fortune has enabled me to fill my days doing what I like best.'

'It seems the height of hypocrisy that a technophobe like yourself should benefit to such an extent from computer shares,' I laughed.

'Mea culpa,' he admitted, 'but as a means to an end it worked out exceptionally well for me.'

'Have you always had a love of colour?' I asked.

'That came about in a very singular manner,' he replied. 'You may recall on our last meeting I spoke briefly of my brother?'

'You did mention he tried to drown you in the bath.'

'Well the fact is – he succeeded.'

'What!' I exclaimed.

'I was clinically dead for a short time.'

'Do you have any recollection of it?'

'Colours, Hopkins – that's what I recollect – a kaleidoscope of colours. That's where my fascination stems from – and I also believe my brain, being starved of oxygen, was affected in some queer way, as it is from that moment I can date my love affair with numbers and all things mathematical. Which brings me to the reason I asked you down here. I daresay you're curious as to that.'

'I was rather intrigued by your call,' I replied.

'I believe I have made a breakthrough in my research.'

'As regards?'

'Numbers being at the bottom of all things.'

'But you said time was at the bottom of all things when last we met.'

'I was wrong.'

These were uncharted waters indeed – in all the years I had known Ormerod I had never heard him own to being wrong about anything.

'Look here,' he said, placing a notebook in my hands.

I did look – to find a bewildering array of mathematical formulae which meant nothing at all to me.

'You forget that I do not share your knowledge of all things numeric,' I said. 'Can you not exhort someone who has at least a basic understanding of the subject to take my part?'

He snatched the book from me and circled a long and complex equation with a red pen.

'There is not a man in the world who would understand this,' he said.

'Perhaps a woman then?' I countered with a smile.

'This is a serious business, Hopkins,' he replied icily.

'But how can I help?'

'By simply being here, observing and taking notes.'

'What exactly is it that you propose to do?' I asked.

'Stop time,' he replied.

I shook my head sadly. 'Good God man – did you hear what you just said?'

'I propose to stop my own personal time – not yours.'

'I am glad of the distinction,' I answered him with some irony. 'Let us suppose – for argument's sake – that you are able to do such a thing. How am I to know it has happened?'

'I cannot say – that is what you are here to observe.'

'There are times I fear for your sanity, Ormerod,' I sighed.

'I assure you I am as sane – or insane – as the next man.'

'How are we to commence then?'

'Just as we are. I will put the equation to work in my box of tricks and we shall see what results.'

So saying, he drew a metal box from a nearby drawer. I

saw it was some electrical contraption, complete with a headpiece composed of individual electrodes.

'But how is that possible?' I argued. 'Are we able to control our own brainwaves?'

He rubbed some gel over his bald pate and put on the headpiece.

'We can all of us exercise such self-control to a certain extent,' he answered. 'But I believe I am in a better position to do so than most – due to my early death. Shall we proceed? If you will just plug me in at the mains please.'

'I am completely at your disposal,' I replied, carrying out his request before taking the pad and pen he offered.

'Excellent – then let us go to it.'

With that he took a deep breath and closed his eyes. The ticking of the clock on his study wall seemed to jeer at our experiment. That, and the sound of a squally shower of rain on the window, was all that broke the silence.

After a few minutes my friend's breathing grew more shallow and his eyes slowly opened. I was alarmed to see that his pupils had turned upwards and were almost invisible. This was the first note I made of events.

At the end of twenty minutes Ormerod's breathing had all but disappeared and I could see no outward movement from his lungs whatsoever. His eyes continued open but there was a constant flickering of his lids which caused me to put pen to paper and make further notes.

I looked up to find that my companion's facial complexion appeared to be growing paler, the flickering of his eyes continuing. Having written my observations my astonishment on returning to the subject in hand is not capable of being expressed by mere words alone.

The fact was that Ormerod's hair was burgeoning forth and his features were growing younger! I watched in a mixture of fascination and amazement as the years continued to fall from my friend's face before my eyes. The process seemed to be gathering pace and my fascination soon turned to horror! Suddenly the box controlling the flow of electric current began to belch forth smoke! Throwing pen and paper aside I rushed across the room, tore the apparatus from his head and grabbing his shoulders I began to shake him violently.

'Ormerod!' I screamed. 'Ormerod! Stop! For the love of God stop man!'

He was twitching uncontrollably with muscular spasms, his mouth agape, his eyes rolling in his head as I continued with my exhortations.

'In God's name man! Stop, for all that's holy!'

At that he gave a deep gasp and gurgle – as a baby being born would – and began muttering incoherently until at last his head slumped forward and I thought him dead. Reaching for the whisky bottle I placed it to his lips and he spluttered into life as he drank it down.

'Great Scott, Ormerod!' I exclaimed. 'What a scare you gave me. Don't ever ask me to watch a repeat performance.'

His head rose slowly from his breast and I saw that sweat was dripping from his forehead – and that he looked twenty years younger than when we had begun.

'Hopkins?' he said groggily. 'Is that you? Good God! What's happened to you?'

'To me?' I replied in astonishment.

'You look so much older!'

We sat through the night. He knew neither where he was nor how he came to be there. I showed him his book of equations – they meant nothing at all to him. Perhaps in twenty years' time they will. In the meantime twenty years have been erased from his memory and he must now live them over.

I thank God I was there with him that evening. Not a day goes by when I don't think with dread of what might have happened had I not been present to shake him out of his trance when I did. But who could I share such thoughts with? Who would believe me?

THE RING

I

'YOU found it?'

'Yes – digging in the garden,' said Ricky.

Bill took the ring from his friend and examined it keenly. 'It's a cracker,' he said.

'Cleaned up good as new,' said Ricky. 'Must be gold, eh?'

'I'd imagine so. Any hallmarks?'

'None that I could see.'

'Probably too old for hallmarks.'

'You reckon?'

'Yes. There's an inscription – but I can't make it out.'

'It's "In aeternum te amabo"' – Latin,' said Ricky. 'I googled it – it means "I will love you for all eternity".'

'It's an incredible find,' said Bill. 'What are you going to do with it?'

'It's Jacqui's birthday next week – I thought I'd buy a little box and give her the ring in it.'

Bill laughed. 'Romantic – and cheap.'

'Do you think she'll like it?'

'I'm sure she'll be all over you when you tell her the translation.'

'I'll let you know how it goes. Another Guinness is it?'

II

'Oh it's gorgeous, Ricky!' squealed Jacqui.

'You like it?'

'I love it! It's so – retro – and so romantic,' she simpered, kissing her husband of six months. 'You're really getting in touch with your feminine side.'

'Better make sure it fits – in case I need to take it back like,' said the bare-faced Ricky, sliding it onto his wife's finger.

'It's perfect!' she screamed. 'Oh Ricky, it's as if it was made for me.'

'Well – I had a fair idea of your size from choosing the wedding ring.'

'You're so thoughtful – and I'll love you for all eternity too,' she added, giving him a slobbery kiss.

'Shall we have some breakfast then?'

'Yes, I'll make it. Do you want a fry-up?'

'That sounds great,' smiled Ricky, sitting down at the kitchen table with the morning paper. 'You got any plans for today?' he asked.

'I'm having lunch with Gemma and Sharon.'

'Thought we might go out for dinner tonight – seeing it's your birthday.'

'Lovely! But where?'

'Dunno – where do you fancy?' asked Ricky.

'D'Argios is nice.'

'You fancy Italian then?'

'Where did I put those eggs?' said Jacqui, poking her head in a cupboard.

'It gets a good name does D'Argios.'

'Have you seen the eggs, Ricky?'

'What, love?'

'Hast thou gone deaf since last we spoke?' snarled Jacqui turning to face him. Ricky smiled and continued reading. 'Thou pig-bellied moldworp! Thou craven, hedge-born jolthead!'

'What the!' exclaimed Ricky, growing paler by the second.

'Canst thou do nothing save lie with thy whey-faced harlot!'

'Jacqui!'

'Well do I know of thy lewdness with the idle-headed, flax-wench whore! Think thee that thou could conceal thy common-kissing, onion-eyed strumpet from me? Hah! How little thou knowest ye pribbling fustilarian! May thou rot in hell with thy bawdy harpy!'

With that, she grabbed a large serrated knife from the kitchen worktop and approached Ricky in what could only be described as a menacing manner.

Ricky, to his credit – and his future – dodged two potentially lethal swipes before planting a right hook on his wife's jaw that immediately despatched her into the Land of Nod. Pulling the birthday ring from her finger he opened the back door and was in the process of throwing it as far as he could when he stopped in his tracks and put it in his pocket.

'What – what happened?' mumbled Jacqui as she started to come round.

'You were looking for eggs and slipped and fell,' said Ricky.

'Oh Ricky – I had the weirdest dream.'

'Never mind – let's get you up and see how you are. That's a sore bruise you'll have there. They'll be saying I put one on you.'

'Oh don't make me laugh,' winced Jacqui with a tortured smile.

'I think we better stay in today. We'll keep D'Argios for next week.'

'I can't remember getting up this morning,' said Jacqui.

'Can't you? And it's your birthday too!'

'So it is! – but what did you get me?'

'I told you – it's a surprise – you'll get it later today.'

'I think I'll go and lie down for a bit.'

'Good idea. Come on – I'll help you upstairs,' said Ricky.

III

'What do you make of this?'

'A bit special. Gold – big ruby too – circa 1580? "In aeternum te amabo" – how romantic! It's quite a find. Where'd you get it?'

'Came in the post this morning.'

'In the post!'

'No letter – just an envelope addressed to the museum with this in it.'

'Phew! Got to be worth eight grand as treasure trove.'

'Maybe someone had a guilty conscience.'

'Oh well – their loss is our gain.'

AN AFTER DINNER STORY

ANNETTE PEARSON'S soirées were always a source of intense pleasure to me. Having made her acquaintance through a mutual friend I was enchanted by the lady immediately and delighted to soon be invited into the inner circle which dined at her house on three or four occasions each year.

Annette was a first-class cook and took great satisfaction in preparing the evening repast. On my first visit I was understandably rather nervous upon arrival, but within the space of a few minutes the assembled guests had put me quite at ease with their warm, friendly welcome. I soon discovered that there was neither bore nor boor among them.

The company varied, but there was a hard core of five who were constantly present. These were Annette, myself, John Richardson, his wife Flora and Henry Strickland. Eight was Annette's perfect dinner party number and so three others were invariably present to make up the party and I never yet felt ill at ease in the company of anyone Annette invited into her home. Conversation was always lively, with wit, jest and intellectual stimulus unfailingly on the evening's menu.

The particular night I wish to speak of was one in which

only the hard core five I mentioned earlier were present. It was a bitter winter's night and I believe the three others who were supposed to join us had been forced to cancel owing to travel difficulties due to the inclement weather.

Being five old friends, the atmosphere was relaxed and intimate. Having polished off an excellent meal, drinks were poured and, in the case of the men at least, trouser belts let out a notch. I believe it was Henry who set the tone of the conversation that ensued …

'As fine a dinner as you've ever cooked,' said Henry.

'Compliments to the chef are certainly due, Annette,' added Flora.

'Oh I'm just glad it all turned out so well,' said our host with a hint of a blush.

'I can't understand why you don't go and find yourself a husband. You certainly know the way to a man's heart,' said Henry with his customary chuckle.

'Are you volunteering?' Annette asked.

'Eh? What!' said the flustered Henry as we all laughed at the discomfit of this self-confessed confirmed bachelor.

'You let yourself in for that one, Henry,' I said. 'But I don't suppose there's the ghost of a chance of gaining access to your heart via your stomach.'

He snapped his fingers sharply. 'Now that's the very thing I propose we discuss tonight,' he said.

'Marriage via the alimentary canal?' I asked.

'No – ghosts.'

'Ghosts?' said Flora sceptically.

'Yes – I was wondering earlier if anyone had ever seen one.'

The assembled company shook their heads and there was a moment's silence until …

'Can't say I have,' said John Richardson. 'Though I did have an odd experience many years ago.'

'Something inexplicable?' asked Henry.

'It was certainly something I personally could find no explanation for.'

'Then it's the very thing we want to hear about!' said Henry excitedly. 'If everyone is in favour?'

We each gave our enthusiastic consent and turned our attention to John as he began to speak.

'I've always been quite a bookish chap and even as a boy I would scour around the local church jumble sales, picking up volumes here and there for threepence or sixpence. At one particular stall I found an old copy of The Strand Magazine – I remember it was dated 1907 – and it looked interesting, so I bought it.'

'It turned out to be full of a wealth of great articles and stories – but what I found even more interesting were the advertisements. There were over eighty pages of them and some of the most incredible contraptions I had ever seen were on view in the illustrations. Nose adjusters, bath chairs, electric shock boxes, cures for baldness, cures for drunkenness – Antidipso that one was called. And stuck in the middle of all this was a little ad for a fountain pen.'

'Now – don't ask me why – but I had wanted a fountain pen since I was knee high to a flea – and of course you know that even now I always carry one.' He took the item from his inside pocket to prove his point. 'The problem was the ones I really wanted were all very expensive.'

'He had expensive tastes even as a boy,' said Flora. 'Not a lot has changed.'

'Pot and kettle springs to mind,' smiled John, 'given what you paid for the outfit you wore to May's wedding.'

'But that was –' Flora began before Henry interrupted her.

'Let's stick with the story if you please. You can battle it out later in the privacy of your home.'

'Well,' said John continuing, 'the point is that the fountain pen in The Strand Magazine ad was only 10/6d – which was well within my means.'

'Yes – but when did you buy the magazine?' asked Annette.

'It must have been about 1966. I'd have been thirteen or fourteen.'

'Surely old enough to know that the shop selling the pens in 1907 would no longer be there?'

'Yes – I suppose I realised that,' laughed John, 'but I just thought it would be fun to try.'

'You sent money to the address?' I asked.

'Yes – a postal order for 10/6d – and a self-addressed envelope which I hoped would ensure its safe return, in the event of the obvious happening.'

'And?' said Annette.

'The pen arrived a week later.'

'I'll be damned!' said Henry.

'I confess I was dumbfounded myself,' said John. 'It came meticulously wrapped in brown paper, string and sealing wax – and there was also a catalogue enclosed, a list of pens, papers, envelopes – all manner of stationery items.'

'And the pen?' asked Henry. 'How was it?' John took the pen from his inside jacket pocket once more. 'Same one? After all these years?'

'Yes – best thing I ever bought,' said John. 'Over forty years' use for 10/6d.'

'I can understand you describing your experience as inexplicable,' said Henry.

'But that wasn't the end of the matter,' said John. 'In the course of the next eighteen months I sent away for various items from the catalogue, all of which found their way through my letterbox. In fact I recall one particular time when I forgot to enclose the remittance and the item still arrived – with a note thanking me for my order and stating that as I was such a regular and valued customer they had despatched the goods to me – but would I please send the money when I had a spare minute – words to that effect.'

'You certainly wouldn't find that happening these days,' said Henry.

'In the course of time this phase of my youth passed and I forgot all about it.'

'It's a pity you didn't follow it up,' said Flora. 'It's such an incredible thing to have happened.'

'Actually I did follow it up – albeit quite by chance many years later,' said John.

We all leaned in closer around the table at his words.

'As you know, I started a career in banking after leaving university and at one point I was sent to London by my employers to take part in one of the many courses such work often entails. Whilst there I had some free time to do some sightseeing and, as I strolled around at my leisure, I suddenly came upon a street sign for Gracemount Place – the very location where I had sent my envelopes all those years ago.'

'Was the shop still there then?' Henry asked excitedly.

'Let John tell the story!' Flora chastised him.

'Of course – sorry – carry on old man.'

'I recalled the number as being 47,' John continued, 'and 47 was indeed still there – but it was now an upmarket shoe shop.'

'Hardly surprising after all those years,' said Flora.

'My thoughts exactly,' said John. 'Nevertheless, I went inside and found the old chap who owned the place to be very polite and only too glad to take a trip down memory lane. When I asked if he remembered the premises being a stationers he informed me that his father had bought the building in the mid-1930s and they had just celebrated forty years there. Previous to his father's purchase a fishmonger had been in residence – though he couldn't say for how long. I thanked him for his time and left with a fine pair of boots which gave me excellent service for a number of years.'

'And that was that then?' said Annette.

'Not quite,' John replied. 'You know what I'm like when I get the bit between my teeth. I was too near the heart of things to just walk away. I was determined to get to the bottom of this conundrum.'

'But how?' asked Flora.

'My next stop was the British Library – where I asked for the bound volume of The Strand Magazine for 1907.'

'Bravo!' said Henry with his habitual chuckle.

'I couldn't recall which month the advert was in, but of course I eventually found it – and the name of the proprietor of the store – a Mr George Edwards. The address was indeed 47 Gracemount Place. I wasn't entirely sure what to do next until the idea of looking up Mr Edwards at the Registry Office came to mind – as it was probable that he not only worked but lived in the building in 1907. The assistant I found at the office was kindness itself and in no time at all she had tracked down her quarry and was able to inform me that George Edwards of 47 Gracemount Place had been killed when the building was bombed in a Zeppelin raid on 31st May 1915.'

'Good God! exclaimed Henry.

'She even found a report of the raid on microfilm – and his obituary. I can assure you all it was a queer feeling to find myself, an hour later, standing in the rain by the gravestone of a man who had been dead for fifty years when he wrote to me in the mid-1960s.'

THE LAST OF ITS KIND

I

'SO, as we can see, pi is an irrational number. Tompkins – what did I just say?'

'Pies and a dash of cucumber, sir.'

'Come here Tompkins.'

Billy Tompkins rose from his desk wearily and trudged to the front of the class.

'Hands out,' said Mr Williams. His strap rose and fell three times. 'Back to your seat, boy.'

Maths was so boring it was no wonder Billy's mind wandered. What did he care about pies? Unless they had meat in them. What good was it to him if circles were round and triangles had three sides? Why couldn't they teach him something useful at school, instead of languages no one spoke any more and how to prove X+Y=Z?

The ring of the bell signalled an end to mathematics for another day.

'Too bad about Old Williams picking on you,' said Billy's friend Peter as they made their way out. Billy shrugged. 'You took it well though.'

'He's not the hardest hitter in the world,' said Billy

nonchalantly, feeling secretly pleased his unconcern at his punishment had been noticed.

'Next couple of hours should be better,' said Peter.

'Science?'

'Yes, but we'll get out – it's the botany field trip to the woods.'

'Oh yes,' said Billy brightening. 'I'd forgotten about that.'

'Least we'll be able to have some fun. Thompson won't be too bothered about us – he never bothers much about anything – 'cept his plants of course.'

Mr Thompson's lax attitude to corporal punishment was another reason his class looked forward to their twice weekly science lesson. They gathered outside the school gates where their teacher was already waiting. Having carried out a head count, Mr Thompson addressed them in his usual benign fashion.

'We are fortunate indeed to have such ancient woodland on our very doorstep, I would ask you to pay particular attention to the flora you will find in abundance during our trip today, and to pick five samples to take back to class in order that we may make a record of them for our ongoing botany project.'

'Picking flowers?' said Peter scornfully. 'No way I'll be doing any of that!'

'Me neither,' said Billy. 'That's cissy stuff. Bound to see some toads and things though.'

'Yes,' said Peter, cheering up. 'Beetles too – bound to be loads of beetles.'

'Come along then,' said their teacher. 'A short walk to the woods and then thirty minutes to collect our samples before we return to class.'

They set off down the road to the wood in a chaotic manner with Mr Thompson in the forefront, blissfully unaware of the anarchic zigzag of pupils that followed in his wake. Upon arrival at their destination he turned and spoke once more.

'Now I want you to follow the path here and don't stray too far off it. We'll walk a short distance into the wood and then you can commence with your task. Is that understood?'

'Yes sir,' they replied with their customary boredom. Billy and Peter were at the back of the straggly line.

'This'll be cool,' said Peter. 'We might get a natterjack.'

'Might be puff balls!' said Billy.

They were walking along a narrow path with a steep drop to a dark, densely wooded area on their left.

'Keep up now,' shouted Mr Thompson – just as Billy tripped over a tree root and fell headlong down the incline.

'Sir! Sir!' shouted Peter.

'What is it?' said their tutor testily, turning abruptly.

'Please sir, Billy Tompkins has fallen down the hill.'

'Stupid boy!' came the contemptuous reply.

II

Billy was aware he was rolling over and over for what seemed forever, when suddenly he came to a precipitous halt and was no longer aware of anything.

When he came to he could smell smoke. Only half conscious, he tried to raise himself up but a firm hand pushed him down again and then supported the back of his head.

'Drink this,' said a voice. He accepted the wooden cup that the slim hand proffered and took a sip. 'More – take more.' This time he gulped what remained and fell back.

He could taste mint and nutmeg. The liquid began to clear the fog in his head. With a groan of pain he propped himself up on one elbow and opened his eyes.

He saw he was in a hut of some sort, a hut made of thatch and twigs, with a small fire burning in the centre and the rising smoke disappearing through a hole in the roof. Before him stood a tall, long-haired, bearded figure dressed in a white robe.

'Are you Jesus?' he asked in awe.

'I am Calmarus,' the stone-faced figure replied.

Disappointing as this news was to Billy he was careful not to show it – as at least it seemed he wasn't dead.

'Where am I?' he asked.

'In the wood of Archeon.' None the wiser, Billy raised a hand to his head and winced. 'Take care,' said his companion. 'I am preparing a poultice for your injury.' With that he turned to the fire and took something from a bowl that was boiling there. Putting it carefully between two large leaves he placed it on Billy's brow.

'Ow! That nips!' squealed Billy.

'It will lessen the swelling. Hold it firmly.'

'Thompson will report me to the rector for this,' said Billy softly. 'Maybe it'll be OK if you speak for me.'

'Speak for you?'

'Yes – to Mr Thompson. I'm sure he'd listen to . . .' Billy's voice trailed off as the knowledge dawned on him that his science teacher might be less than impressed by the bearded, white-robed hippy type. 'Do you live here?'

'This is my dwelling.'

'Who did you say you are?'

'I am Calmarus.'

'Karl Morris? Well look, Karl – I'll need to get back to school – I'm already in serious bother.'

'You must rest awhile,' said Calmarus.

'I don't have time to rest!' said the exasperated Billy, trying to get up.

The firm hand held him in place. 'There is no time here.'

'No time?' laughed Billy looking at his watch. 'Why it's –' He gave the glass a tap with his finger and shook his arm. 'It seems to have stopped – battery must be dead.'

Calmarus removed the poultice from Billy's head and placed his hand there. Seemingly satisfied, he took some white powder from a small leather bag which was hanging by his side and smeared it on the boy's brow.

'Ooh! That's really great!' sighed Billy immediately. 'The pain just disappeared! Are you a doctor?'

'I am a Druwide.'

'A Druid? What – like at Stonehenge?'

'I am Calmarus, last of the Druwides of the Britaini.'

'Last?' said Billy. 'Where did all the rest go?'

His companion's face grew sad. 'Their souls departed

when the invaders assailed us that fateful day on the island of Mona.'

'It must be pretty cool being a Druid – standing at the stones on Midsummer Day. How do you get to be one?'

'I studied for twenty years – here and in Gaul.'

'Twenty years!' yelped Billy. 'I don't think my mum would be too happy about that – though she does hope I'll spend four at university – not that I can see that happening.'

Calmarus laid his hand on Billy's forehead once more. 'Now you are well,' he pronounced.

'So it's OK to go?'

'Yes, it is time for you to go.'

'It's been jolly good of you to help me,' said Billy getting to his feet.

'The pleasure is mine,' said Calmarus. 'It is good to use one's art to some purpose.' He led the boy to the doorway and they stepped outside.

'Damn!' said Billy. The Druid gave a questioning look. 'I'm supposed to collect five plants for Thompson's stupid botany project – and I haven't got any!'

Calmarus walked a few paces to the trees and plucked a small white flower that was growing among them. 'Take this,' he said.

Billy accepted it with good grace. 'I suppose one is better than none at all,' he smiled.

The Druid pointed to a dim path nearby. 'Follow the road and it will lead you to your friends,' he said, placing his hand on Billy shoulder and urging him onwards.

The boy walked a few paces and then looked back to wave a farewell – only to see a vista of ancient woodland. 'Must have walked further than I thought,' he mused quietly, far from convinced by the statement.

'He's here, sir! I've found him!! shouted Peter as Billy came in view. 'You OK?'

'Sure,' said Billy. 'Get any toads?'

'Not yet – plenty of time left though.'

Billy looked at his watch. It was ticking again and showed they still had twenty-five minutes of their thirty left. 'That's weird,' he said.

'What is?' asked Peter.

'Oh – nothing – nothing important.'

'Tompkins!' shouted his out of breath science master, puffing his way up to meet the boys. 'Enjoy your trip, what?' he said, laughing at his own joke.

'Yes sir – sorry sir.'

'Well, well – no harm done. No broken bones, eh?'

'No sir.'

'Well carry on – carry on – but I see you've already got a specimen, Tompkins.'

'Yes sir,' said Billy, holding out the flower Calmarus had given him.

Mr Thompson's mouth opened and he moved his spectacles from the tip of his nose closer to his eyes. 'Good God!' he exclaimed. Not content with that, he repeated himself – only it took twice as long to say it. 'Good – God!' He took the white flower from Billy's hand and both boys later swore they saw tears in the old man's eyes.

'Epigogium Aphyllum,' he whispered. 'The ghost orchid.' His gaze shifted to Billy – who saw that they were tears of joy. 'Do you know how long this flower has been extinct?'

SCRAPS OF LIFE

'HOW did you get involved in the first place?' asked Jones.

'They'd bought the house at auction – contents and all – and there was a pile of old books there, so Davidson's wife asked me if I'd run a semi-professional eye over them to see if there was anything of value before they threw them out,' Watts replied, draining his glass of brandy before refilling both his own and his companion's.

'Is that Margaret?'

'Yes – we worked together in Latimer's for a few years.'

'Then you knew her before you knew Davidson?'

'I knew them both. I introduced them to each other.'

'A regular matchmaker,' said Jones with a grin.

'I've often regretted it,' Watts replied ruefully. 'I should have kept her for myself.'

'Are they happy?' Watts shook his head silently and sipped at his glass. 'So why the house move?'

'It wasn't a move. Davidson had plans to turn it into flats – student accommodation, being near the university you see.'

'Did he have experience in that field?'

'No,' said Watts contemptuously. 'I think he'd watched one too many house renovations on TV and decided he could do it as well as any of them.'

'And Margaret went along with it?'

Watts sighed. 'So it would seem. Davidson can be quite convincing at times. I always considered there to be a touch of the manic depressive about him – he's all peaks and troughs.'

'So you went to the house to look at those books?'

'No, no – I was nowhere near the house at that stage. Everything had been cleared out and put into storage – prior to being sold off to the first person who would make any kind of offer for it.'

'Nothing of value then?'

'Bits and bobs – nothing much.'

'Seems a bit strange – to buy a house including contents if you don't want them.'

'That was the deal,' Watts replied with a shrug. 'I learned later the old woman who had lived there had died and her only living relative, a niece, was in New Zealand. She just wanted the cheque with a minimum of hassle.'

'No Ian Fleming first editions in the bookcase then?'

'No bookcase! They were all in filing cabinets. Nothing of any worth – mostly book club editions from the 1950s.'

'But you found the scrapbook there?'

'Yes,' Watts replied. 'That's it on the table – feel free to have a look.'

'Did Davidson say anything about it?' asked Jones, rising and picking up the volume.

'When I told him I was interested he said I could take whatever I liked.'

'Pretty decent of him – maybe you should have taken Margaret.'

'Well – as I said – peaks and troughs. Must have caught him on a good day.'

'What exactly am I looking at here?' said a puzzled Jones. 'It seems to be newspaper reports of missing teenage girls from the 1920s.'

'That's it in a nutshell. Seemed weird – that's what drew me to it,' Watts replied.

'Fairly extensive I must say. Paris, Vienna, London, New Jersey.'

'One in Mosshill too.'

'Really?'

'Page nineteen.'

Jones flicked his fingers over the paper. 'So there is! Catherine Burns – aged sixteen. Disappeared from 42 Dryad Street, Mosshill – but surely that's the –'

'– address of the house Davidson bought? Yes, it is.'

'This is starting to get interesting.'

'That's what I thought at the time,' said Watts.

'Very neatly done,' said Jones as he continued to turn over the pages. 'So symmetrical and easy on the eye. The only writing appears to be the numbers under each report – here's 10/32, 9/8, 12/88 – any idea what they signify?'

'What's underneath Catherine Burns?' asked Watts.

Jones worked his way backwards. '7/11,' he said.

'Davidson bought the house in mid-June last year.'

'And?' Jones frowned.

'And the problem appeared three weeks later.'

'I'm not quite sure I – oh you mean 7/11 – the month and the year!' Jones exclaimed as the penny dropped.

'None of the first numbers are higher than twelve – so I thought it was a safe bet that they were dates – it was just a bit of a conundrum as to why they should be there.'

'But surely you had done your bit – looked at the books, given your opinion and then left the entrepreneurs to it.'

'That's precisely what I did – and I didn't expect to hear any more about it – until Margaret called me about a month later.'

'In July?'

'In July – the 5th to be precise.'

'Is she prone to calling you?'

'Not at all – a text on my birthday and at Christmas keeps us in some kind of touch though.'

'Then it must have been something important for her to call.'

'It was certainly a bit of a shock to hear her voice,' said Watts. 'Though the first thing she did was apologise for phoning me – as it was really a police matter.'

'Police? Burglary was it?' asked Jones.

'She wouldn't say any more – just asked if I could please come and join her at the new house – where she was busy painting the walls.'

'Seems a reasonable enough request.'

'It does – other than the police matter part.'

'So you went?'

'Yes – she was looking for me out of the window as I arrived and seemed tense when she opened the door – apologising again. I asked her what it was all about and she led me into a room which was empty except for a young girl sitting on a wooden chair.'

'Who's this?' I asked, turning to Margaret. 'Cathy Burns,' says the girl – like a tape recorder being switched on. 'She just turned up this morning,' says Margaret. 'Walked in and sat down saying this is her home. I can't get anything else out of her.'

Jones gave a low whistle. 'Catherine Burns! Same age as when she disappeared?'

'She looked sixteen to me.'

'Would have a telegram from the Queen by now if it's the same girl. What did you do?'

'I asked her when she was born.'

'And?'

'Tape recorder went on again and she said 1908.'

'Incredible!'

'Scary.'

'How was she dressed – Edwardian?'

'No – modern teenage clothes.'

'I can understand it putting the wind up you.'

'Margaret said she was going to phone the police – but her fingers had dialled my number instead.'

'What – against her will?'

'Apparently so.'

'You do have all the fun, Watts.'

'Fun? Didn't seem like fun to me. The girl was just sitting there – motionless, expressionless – like a life-size marionette. I asked her where she lived and she replied, "42 Dryad Street." I asked her what year it was. She said,

"1924". I asked her where she had come from. She replied, "Orion".'

'Orion?' said Jones.

'That's what she said – Orion.'

'What else did you ask her?'

'Didn't get the chance – there was a knock at the door. I went to answer it and found a well-dressed young man in a black suit, with the clearest ice-blue eyes I've ever seen. He fixes me with those eyes – like I'm a bullseye in a target – and with a big smile says he believes his sister may have entered my house in error.'

'He said, in error?'

'Yes.'

'An educated young man?'

'He had a bit of an accent, but I couldn't place it. After that he tells me about her mental health issues and apologises for the inconvenience – and somehow he's edged his way through the door and in front of me. "Carly!" he beams when he sees the girl.'

'Carly? I thought it was Cathy,' said Jones.

'That's what I said to him – but she's got multiple personalities according to her brother.'

'Did you catch his name?' asked Jones.

'No – but I asked him what Carly was doing here and before he could answer she said, "Babies".'

'Babies?' said Jones.

'Brother just laughed – he seemed to think the whole thing was a spiffing wheeze – mental health issues, multiple personalities, babies – it was all just one big jolly to him.'

'How did Margaret take it all?'

Not for the first time Watts shrugged his shoulders. 'What could she – or I – do?'

'You let them go?'

'They were hardly prisoners.'

'All the same –'

Both men sipped at their drinks.

'He wasn't a man to be trifled with,' said Watts quietly.

They sipped some more.

'So what do you make of it?' Jones asked.

Watts lit a cigarette and took a long draw on it. 'I can't make it all out,' he said.

'But can you make some of it out?'

'An imagination like mine fills in gaps – with whatever nonsense takes its fancy.'

'Go on then,' Jones urged.

Watts sighed and scratched his head. 'Let's start with the fact that all these girls certainly disappeared – as evinced by ocular verification in the scrapbook.'

'Nicely put – but no awards from the Plain English Society.'

'Now – what do you associate Orion with?'

'A car? Someone with a belt in Greek mythology?'

'Yes – Orion's Belt.'

'A star constellation!'

'So put a distant star constellation and missing teenage girls together and what do you get?'

'Alien abduction!' they said as one.

'You're right about your imagination,' Jones laughed. 'But where do the babies fit in?'

'Sci-fi films generally have hordes of alien spaceships blasting the hell out of New York in their bid to conquer Earth,' said Watts. 'But what if that's not the way it would really be? What if they abduct young girls – and genetically alter them so that any offspring are –'

'– Alien?' said Jones.

'Alien – in keeping with their idea of conquering Earth slowly, but surely, over centuries – millennia perhaps.'

'And those dates below the newspaper reports?'

'That's when they get sent back.'

'This century?'

'Who knows – maybe – or maybe 12/88 means December 2588. All we have to go on is Cathy.'

'But if they all turned up where they originally disappeared then it would be a waste of time.'

'Certainly. But the thing is – we always associate aliens with infallibility. What if they make mistakes sometimes?'

'Mistakes?'

'What if Cathy is a mistake. Her mind is supposed to be no longer her own – yet something remains – some memory that brings her here. What if she requires a bit of fine tuning and a mechanic is sent down to take her in for a tune-up?'

'Her brother you mean?'

'Yes.'

What an idea! And you suggest that all these girls are placed back into the world simply to procreate and raise a family of extra-terrestrials?'

'It's just a thought.'

'And what a thought! But what about the scrapbook? How do you explain that? The dates mean that only an alien could have produced it.'

'I didn't say I had an answer for everything,' said Watts, draining his glass.

'I'm glad to hear it,' Jones replied.

'But here on Earth there are always those who are prepared to go against the system – in the name of humanity.'

'Are you now suggesting an alien who has read the Geneva Convention?'

Watts shrugged his shoulders for a final time. 'Maybe there are some who believe in the United Federation of Planets prime directive,' he mused.

PLAY UP AND PLAY THE GAME

'I need something old!' sobbed Leanne.

'I'd have thought Ryan would have covered that,' said her mother fixing a slight crease in her daughter's wedding dress, 'being seven years older than you.'

'You never liked Ryan,' wailed Leanne. 'Just because he made a mistake once in his life.'

'Two years for aggravated assault is a big mistake to make.'

'I've got the new, borrowed and blue stuff – but I must have something old!' her daughter chimed in quickly in a bid to change the subject.

Molly, her long suffering mother, turned to her young son.

'Paul, go upstairs and bring down something out of Uncle Jack's box.'

'The one in the wardrobe?' said the astonished pageboy-in-waiting.

'Yes.'

'The one I'm never allowed to touch?'

'Yes.'

He ran upstairs as fast as his legs could carry him. The wardrobe was already lying open and he quickly pulled the old tin box out of its corner and sat down on the bed with it. The contents had long been a source of fascinating speculation for his imagination and he was trembling with excitement as he pushed back the lid and looked inside. It was a fine preparation for life in general – as he found himself sadly disappointed by the whole spectacle. There was a tattered hymn book, a set of corporal's stripes, an old faded telegram and a tarnished brass whistle.

'Paul! Bring something out of that box now!'

'I'm coming!' he shouted. Grabbing at the whistle he closed up the box and was on his way out when a voice stopped him in his tracks.

'Where are you going with that?'

He wheeled round to find a young man in an army uniform standing by the window.

'I've to give it to our Leanne.'

'Do you know what that is?'

'It's a whistle.'

'But do you know when that whistle was last blown?'

'No,' said Paul.

'Well sit down and I'll tell you boy.'

'I can't – I've got to give this to Mum.'

'There's enough time for that,' smiled the young soldier.

'Are you Uncle Jack?' asked Paul.

'I'm Jack alright.'

'My mum says you were in the war.'

'Your mum's right.'

'What's it like in the war?' Paul asked, with the naivety that only a seven-year-old can have.

Jack's face grew gloomy, 'Not nice, son – not nice at all.'

'Why'd you go there then?'

'I dunno,' laughed Jack. 'Everyone else was going and I didn't want to be left behind.'

'Did they give you this whistle when you went to war?'

'You sit down there and I'll tell you about that whistle.'

Paul sat on the bed and Jack began his story. 'I ain't got a lot of time – so I'll make this short.'

'– And I need to give this to Mum.'

'Well – I was in the trenches during the war – like millions of others.'

'What's trenches?' asked Paul.

'Big long holes that you stand in.'

'Why?'

'That's a good question – and I don't know as I've got an answer for it – but that's the way it was. We were in our trenches and a little way off, the Germans were in their trenches.'

'War sounds silly,' said Paul matter-of-factly.

'It is, son – very silly.'

'What did you do in the trenches?'

'I got lost.'

'Lost?'

'Yes – I got separated from my regiment, the 52nd Lowland Division, and had no idea where I was. Could have been in no man's land heading in the wrong direction for all I knew.'

'Where's that?'

'That's what they called the space between our trenches and the German trenches.'

'I think I understand – if you were lost you might easily have gone to the German trenches and been shot at.'

'You've got it in a nutshell, young fella. But as luck would have it, I ended up in a trench full of Royal Welsh Fusiliers.'

'Did they give you the whistle?'

'They did not – but they gave me some bully beef and a packet of cigarettes.'

'My mum says smoking's a filthy habit.'

'Your mum sounds like a wise lady.'

'But I know she sometimes smokes.'

'A wise sinner is the best of all,' laughed Jack. 'But I was glad to get a smoke and find myself among friends – it was Christmas Eve you see.'

'Did Santa visit the trenches?'

'Course he did!'

'Our Leanne says Santa isn't real – that it's Mum and Dad who buy the presents.'

'Shame on her! Those elves work all year round so Santa can deliver all those presents.'

'What did he bring you?'

'He brought me peace, my boy – the greatest gift of all.' Paul fell silent as Jack went on. 'Yes – it was a cold and frosty Christmas Eve in northern France – near the village of Laventie, as I had just learned, with the Germans only 100 yards away – and as we stood there in the darkness we could hear them singing Silent Night – in their own language of course – but the tune was the same.'

'I know that one,' said Paul and he began to sing. 'Silent night, holy night.'

'That's the one. It was lovely to hear and in return we started to sing Good King Wenceslas.'

'Good King Wenceslas looked out on the Feast of Stephen,' sang Paul.

'You know them all,' laughed Jack. 'We heard the Germans clapping their hands and we clapped ours too and before we knew it we were out the trench all clapping each other in no man's land and somehow we moved forward and they moved forward and we were all there together shaking hands and wishing each other the compliments of the season.'

'I thought you hated each other – isn't that what war is?' said a bemused Paul.

'It's a funny old thing – we found out they were just like us and they found out we were just like them. Next thing I know someone's standing beside me with a football asking if they fancy a kick about.'

'In no man's land?'

'In no man's land! Well Jerry's certainly up for it – but one of them produces the very thing you're holding in your hand.'

'The whistle?'

'Yes – he brings the whistle out of his pocket and we eventually understand that he wants a referee. One of our gang tries to take it from him but he's having none of it. He wants a neutral referee – not an English one – even though they are all Welsh. Then he sees me and points to my Glengarry bonnet. 'Scottish?' he says and I nod my head. He knows his history – knows Scots have a reputation for hating the English even more than they hate the Germans – he reckons I can be trusted to be neutral and he gives me the whistle.'

'Did you send anyone off?'

Jack laughed. 'It was fifty a side and a free for all. I blew it once to start things off and that was that. We'd been playing for half an hour when this Major appeared and ordered us back to our trench, telling us we're supposed to be killing Huns not making friends with them. We were no sooner back than our artillery started up and the shells began flying as usual.'

'You shouldn't have done what the Major said.'

'No,' sighed Jack. 'We shouldn't have done a lot of things.'

A silence came over both of them till Jack gave a long, sharp intake of breath and said, 'You better take that whistle down to your mum.'

'It feels more important now,' said Paul looking at it. 'Now I know what it did – it feels more important than Leanne's stupid wedding.' He lifted his head to look at Jack – only to find he was alone in the room.

'Paul! Bring something down now!' came his mother's voice.

'Coming!' he cried, jumping down the stairs.

'What kept you up there?' Leanne scolded.

'I was talking to Uncle Jack.'

'Never mind Uncle Jack,' she returned absent-mindedly. 'What have you got? A whistle?'

'That'll do lovely,' said Molly as he handed it to his sister.

'Who was Uncle Jack anyway?' asked Leanne, fixing her tiara.

'I think he was your granddad's, granddad's brother – or something like that,' Molly replied.

'Was he in the war?'

'Yes.'

'Which one?'

'I can't remember,' said Molly. 'One of those wars in nineteen canteen I think. Right Paul – time to get your suit on.'

RIGHT SAID FRED

'MUST 'ave been some grand parties 'ere, eh Fred?' said Charlie Cuthbert looking around the stately home in which they were standing.

'Makes you wonder wot 'appened,' said Fred.

'Deaf dooties.'

'You wot?'

'Deaf dooties, Fred – couldn't pay 'em – so they 'ad to sell everyfink in the 'ouse.'

'Shame.'

'Still – it's puttin' bread on our table, mate – and speakin' of tables, let's find this billiard room. I 'eard it's upstairs.'

The billiard room was soon located.

'Look at that,' said Fred. 'Full-size table!'

'Seen better days,' said Charlie sticking his finger through a hole in the green baize.

'Yeah – and it'll see worse by the time we get it out of 'ere.'

'We'll never get it through the door, Fred.'

His companion took off his cap and scratched his head.

'You got a point there, Charlie – I reckon we'll 'ave to saw the legs off first.'

'Reckon you're right – I'll go get the gear.'

The legs were quickly despatched, but problems still beset the pair.

'Watch your end, Charlie!'

'Watch your bloody own, mate!' Fred replied warmly.

'I'm only sayin' – no need to get stroppy.'

'Hmph! Get it on its side.'

'Jesus! It's a ton weight,' said Charlie struggling to turn it upright.

'So what'll we do now?' asked Fred when they were finally holding it sideways. 'We'll never get this down the stairs.'

'You're right, mate – we'll 'ave to go to Plan B.'

'Plan B? Wot the bloody 'ell's that then?'

'On your left,' said Charlie, cocking his head in that direction.

'You wot? Through the winder?

'You got a better idea?'

'We're 20 feet up!'

'It's gettin' tossed anyway – won't matter 'ow many bits it's in.'

'Right,' said Fred with a sigh. 'Let's get it over wiv.'

The deed having been done, they marched downstairs to survey the damage.

'Wot a bloody mess,' said Fred as they stood by the smashed remains. 'We'll need to tidy all this up and put it in the van.'

'Well you better go get it – I ain't carryin' all this round the front,' said Charlie.

'OK – OK – keep yer 'air on – I'll bring it round.'

''Ere – wait a minute – wot's that there?' said Charlie brushing aside a piece of the ripped green baize. 'There's sumfink drawn on it.'

'Where?'

'On the slate – look – where it's cracked open there.'

'Oh yeah,' said Fred peering closer. 'I reckon it's one of 'em fossils, Charlie – look – there's feathers.'

'Fossils?'

'Yeah – it's some ainshunt bird – I read about 'em.'

'I been out with 'em!' laughed Charlie.

'Let's see if we can split the rest of this 'ere slate – you got the 'ammer an' chisel?'

'In the van.'

'Go get 'em then.'

Within an hour they had revealed a perfect specimen of the fossilised bird.

'Big bugger, eh Fred?'

'Six foot – and look at those gnashers. I tell you wot, Charlie – we're on a nice little earner 'ere.'

'You reckon?'

'It's a sure thing – people pay top dollar for stuff like this.'

'Wot you plannin' on doin' wiv it?'

'Well – all we wus told was to get rid of the billiard table. Technically it's ours – as is any fossils found inside.'

'So – we get it in the van?'

'We get it in the van, mate – double quick.'

It proved to be easier said than done – but eventually the pair succeeded in their task.

'Wot about the rest of the stuff?' asked Charlie.

'It ain't goin' nowhere – we can come back for it tomorrow,' Fred replied. 'Let's get this 'ome – we can store it in your garage.'

'My garage!'

'Well it's bigger than mine – and it's got bugger all in it.'

'I'm not sure as Maggie will be too pleased to see it.'

'She needn't see nuffink. 'We'll 'ave it out and in before she knows yer 'ome.'

'So what's your plans for it?'

Fred tapped the side of his nose. 'I got some contacts, Charlie – you just leave it with your old uncle Fred and we'll be alright, mate.'

'Nice bit of fish, Mags,' said Charlie.

'You like it?'

'Yeah – nice.'

'Fresh is it?'

'I'll say it is.'

'I thought it was – being pink like – that shows it's fresh.'

'Mmm,' said Charlie, his mouth full.

'Who's ringin' at this time?' said Maggie angrily, rising to answer the phone.

''Ello? Wot? No! When? Wot happened? No!'

'Wassup?' said Charlie.

'It's Fred,' said Maggie with her hand over the receiver.

'What's he want then?'

''E's dead!'

'Dead? Whadcha mean 'e's dead? I just dropped him off 'ome down the road.'

'This is Judy – Fred's dead!'

'Gimme that phone!' cried Charlie grabbing it from his wife's hand.

'What's this all about Fred being dead?' he shouted down the line before listening in silence for two minutes.

'Well I'll be right over, Judy – I'm on me way now, girl,' he said and put the phone down.

'What 'appened?' asked Maggie.

'That's what I'm goin' to find out.'

'What did Judy say?'

'She said Fred went to the shop to get some ciggies and was 'ardly out the door than he was wavin' at the air and screamin' like a madman.'

''Ee ain't never been prone to turns has Fred.'

'This weren't no turn. People in the street were tryin' to 'elp him – they said he were terrified. Doc says he'd 'ad an 'eart attack.'

'Poor Fred – and Judy of course.'

'I'm goin' over to see wot I can do.'

'I'll just tidy up a bit and come over too.'

'Yeah – Judy'll appreciate that – I'll see you when you get there.'

With that he walked out the front door.

He was aware of the shadow before he reached the street. Looking up he saw the bird's leathery wings flapping awkwardly then heard its hideous screech as it dived down towards him. Soon his own arms were flailing wildly and he himself was screaming like a madman as he fought for his life with a six-foot pterosaur. He saw a passer-by looking at him strangely before moving to the other side of the road – the bird was obviously invisible to all but him.

Charlie soon realised this was a battle he could not win. His strength began to wane and sweat was blinding him when suddenly an idea came to him. He gave it only a one in a hundred chance of success – but it was the only chance he had.

With his invisible prehistoric assailant goading, pecking and biting at him all the way, he fought a path to the garage where the slate fossil stood up against the wall just inside the door. Beside it lay his hammer and chisel. As the bird drew its head back in preparation for a fresh assault, Charlie saw his opportunity and throwing himself into the garage he grabbed the hammer and smashed the slate into a thousand fragments. His nightmare was immediately over.

As he sat amidst the debris shaking from the terror of his experience and with what felt like litres of adrenalin pumping through his body he heard the front door open and slam shut.

'Wot you doin' sat down there? Oh well – come on – shift yer arse – we can both go together now.'

MADAME PISANESCHI

'COME on!' shouted Janet. 'Let's have a go on the waltzers.'

'You paying then?' said Steve.

'Not bloody likely!'

'You're becoming a bit too high-maintenance for me,' her boyfriend replied with a smile, putting his hand in his pocket.

The fairground was teeming with people of all ages. After the waltzers, Steve won Janet a teddy bear by knocking down three tin cans.

'Ooh – he's so cuddly,' she said, pressing the toy to her cheek.

'You what? More than me?'

'Never,' she laughed giving Steve a kiss.

The air was a strange brew of scents. Candy floss, whelks, hamburgers, hot dogs and cigarette smoke.

'Three darts – score less than nineteen to win!' shouted a swarthy young gypsy from his stall.

'You want to try that?' asked Janet.

'Nah. Course if it was over a hundred and twenty you had to score I'd be happy to.'

Dusk was beginning to fall as the couple walked hand in hand to the perimeter of the fair.

'You want to go?' said Janet.

'We'll wait a bit yet,' Steve replied lighting a cigarette. They continued their walk in easy silence, her head resting on his shoulder.

'That's a bloody strange place to put a stall,' said Steve suddenly, pointing to the light of a lone hut far removed from the hub of activity.

'There's a sandwich board outside – let's go and see what it says,' Janet replied.

On approaching and reading it they both burst out laughing.

Madame Pisaneschi – Fortunes Told – £1000

'Costs a fortune to tell your fortune,' Janet chortled.

'Must be a mistake,' said Steve. 'Probably a tenner and she's missed out the dot. Let's go in and see.'

'Not me!' said Janet, pulling back with a frown. 'You know I don't like that kind of stuff.'

'What do you mean?'

'Telling the future and that.'

'It's all bollocks,' said Steve scornfully. 'It's just a bit of fun.'

'You go if you like – I'll wait here,' said Janet, sitting down on a low wall. Give us a fag before you go.'

'I'll see if she'll take a cheque – I've got twenty quid in my account,' said Steve with a wink and a wide-boy grin as he marched up to the hut door and gave it a couple of sharp raps.

'Come in,' came a voice from within.

'We're in,' whispered Steve, blowing his girl a kiss.

Janet giggled nervously and puffed on her cigarette. 'Don't be too long,' she said. 'It's getting dark now.'

'I'll be back before you know it,' said her beau, turning the handle and entering.

Madame Pisaneschi was sitting on a chair reading a paperback book with a bottle of vodka within easy reach. She looked up as Steve came in.

'Yes?' she asked.

'I didn't think you'd need to ask what I wanted – seeing as how you can see the future.'

'I can't see nothing,' she replied.

'What?' said Steve.

'It ain't me as sees,' Madame replied obliquely. 'You looking to get your fortune told?'

'Maybe – but they've made a mistake on your sign – it says £1000.'

'That's right,' she replied.

'You what? A grand!'

'You want quality you has to pay for it.'

'Who's got that kind of money to come in here?'

'Have you?' the gypsy asked.

As his eyes grew more accustomed to the dim light he could see that the fortune teller was no aged crone but a handsome thirty-something woman dressed in the usual paraphernalia associated with her vocation.

'Is it worth it?' he enquired.

'Depends,' she replied.

'Depends on what?'

'On whether you like to hear the truth.'

'I ain't scared,' he said, drawing himself up to full height.

'No?'

'No!' he spat defiantly.

'Well you should be,' she answered quietly.

Steve sat down opposite her. 'You take a cheque?'

Her lips slowly spread into a wry smile. 'Yes – I'll take a cheque alright – upfront.'

He drew a chequebook from his pocket and began to write. 'Who should I make it out to?' he asked.

'Madame P. Pisaneschi,' she replied. 'P-I-S-A-N-E-S-C-H-I.'

He signed it with a flourish, ripped it out and handed it to her. Her eyes sparkled with mirth as she folded it and placed it down her bosom.

'So what do I get for that?' asked Steve. 'Where's your crystal ball?'

'I ain't got one.'

'How do you expect to tell my fortune without a crystal ball then?' he retorted scornfully.

'The spirits will tell me,' she replied.

'Gorn!' Steve laughed. 'The ones in the bottle?' he said, nodding to the vodka. 'Or is it dead spirits you mean?'

'Ain't no live ones,' she answered deadpan.

They eyed each other across the table.

'Go on then,' said Steve breaking the silence. 'What have the spirits got to say about me?' His voice was heavy with sarcasm.

Madame Pisaneschi closed her eyes. A siren could be heard sounding in the distance. Steve gave an involuntary shiver and pulled his jacket round him more tightly. The lamp on the table flickered and Steve saw there was a candle within it. The gypsy woman's eyes opened and she reached for her glass of vodka and drank from it.

'Your uncle Bill's here,' she said.

Steve was momentarily taken aback. It was true he did have a deceased uncle by that name – but he soon reverted to his previous demeanour.

'Everybody's got an uncle Bill,' he said with a curl of his lip.

Madame P. cocked her head to the right as if she was listening to someone. 'He says you've got some money coming to you –' Steve laughed at the hackneyed turn events were taking. 'But you won't have it long.'

'Is that the best you can do?' he sneered.

'And he says you better stop messing about with her at number 42 or Janet's going to know all about it soon.'

Steve's mouth dropped open and the colour drained from his cheeks.

'And he says you better buck up your ideas before it's too late. You've to remember what he used to tell you – you've got to get things done – not bloody talk about doing them.'

'You … you …' gasped Steve.

'And he says you've to get Janet home now because her mum's worried about her being out so late.'

Steve rose unsteadily from his chair. 'How, how do you know these things?' he said fearfully.

'I don't know nothing, love – I just repeat what I'm told.' She took a swig from her glass and locked her eyes onto his. 'You get your money's worth?' she asked.

Steve backed up to the door and turned the handle. 'You're a witch!' he cried in awe.

'Not me, love – no cats or broomsticks in here. Come back anytime,' she smiled.

He turned from her and slammed the door behind him.

'You alright?' said Janet jumping from the wall to greet him. 'You look a bit peaky.'

'Let's go,' he said quietly. 'It's time I got you home.'

Postscript

'Where are we going?' asked Janet.

'Here!' said Steve walking her into the bank.

'Is this the surprise?' she said in disappointment.

'No – this is the surprise.' He pulled a letter from his coat pocket. 'Look – I got my bursary – £990! We're going to party!'

'Ooh!' she cried excitedly. 'Can we go to Romero's for dinner?'

'Course we can,' he laughed, giving her a kiss.

'Next please,' said the teller.

'I got this letter,' said Steve passing it through the grille. 'It says the money's going straight into my account. I'd like it all out please.'

The bespectacled male teller pressed a few buttons on his keyboard. 'I'm afraid there's only £10 in the account,' he said.

'What! Hasn't the money gone in then?' said Steve angrily.

'Oh yes,' came the reply. 'The money has certainly gone in – but a cheque for £1000 has come off since.'

THE KING OF THE GULLS

ON a frosty morning at the start of December, Bob Graham was in the kitchen preparing breakfast and mimicking the nurse who had given him a health check the previous day.

'Cholesterol – 6.28, Mr Graham – we'll have to do something about that.'

He cut the rind off three rashers of bacon.

'Hmph! Bloody cholesterol indeed. Who invented that anyway? Can't even get to enjoy a bit of bacon in peace these days,' he muttered as he was about to throw the three strips of fat in the pedal bin. But then again, he thought – taking his foot off the pedal, so to speak – might as well let some poor creature have the benefit of it.

Opening the back door he threw it onto the roof of his garden hut. Almost immediately two pigeons flapped down and it took the place of the early worm in their diet.

'Hope you enjoyed that,' said Bob. 'Don't suppose you have to worry about your cholesterol level.'

Being 52, unemployed and widowed with no children – or none he was aware of – meant Bob felt he had a good deal to worry about. He closed the door and switched on the TV.

'... House repossessions reached a five-year high in

November …' the smiling female newsreader informed him.

'And I'll be added to the list next year the way things are going,' he concluded gloomily.

Day followed day and each morning the fat from his bacon rashers made its way onto the garden hut. The scuffles of the birds as they fought over it made Bob think of human scuffles. After a week the squabbling pigeons were supplanted by squabbling seagulls and no other bird species subsequently appeared. The gulls were too big and brutal for mere pigeons or magpies to contend with.

The 20th December was a particularly cold day and yet Bob stood for longer than usual at the back door that morning. Across the street a line of seagulls sat perched on the roofs of the houses opposite, yet only one flew down to partake of that morning's food. It struck Bob as being strange – until the smoke alarm brought him back indoors to his burnt rashers under the grill.

As time went by it became apparent that this was the shape of things to come. The row of birds sat patiently each morning until one lone gull glided down for the meal. Are they taking turns? thought Bob. One gull looks much the same as another. He began to pay closer attention, seeking a distinguishing mark – and he found one – a small black spot near the tail. It was the same bird each day, he was sure of it. 'Strange, strange, strange,' he mused.

The gull and he eyed each other each morning. In the middle of February Bob decided to try and coax it closer.

One day instead of throwing the bacon rind onto the hut, he left it on the bottom back step. The bird glided down as usual and landed on the garden shed. From there it flew onto the lawn then proceeded cautiously towards the steps. Bob was standing on the top one. The beady-eyed gull looked up at him and then moved forward quickly and snapped up its meal before flying off. Next morning Bob left the fat on the second bottom step and there was a repeat performance. Gulls were big buggers when you got up close to them and it was a toss-up which was more wary – Bob or the bird.

The end of the week found Bob feeling brave. He sat on the top step with the fat held out in his outstretched palm – and adrenalin flowing freely through his body.

The gull landed a few feet off and cocked its head to the side. Slowly, by almost imperceptible degrees, it edged closer and closer to him, stopping at the bottom step for what seemed an age. Finally it made the decision to hop up first one step then another. Bob held his breath – he'd never been this close to such a large gull. SNAP! Its beak moved like lightning and the fat was gone – as was the bird. Bob's face creased into a huge smile – he felt like a lion tamer.

June 21st dawned warm and sunny. The gull snapped up the food from his fingers, as was now normal, and Bob thought that was that for another day – but he was wrong.

No sooner had the bird landed on the roof opposite than all those hangers-on around it flew down and landed on the lawn leaving Bob's visitor a solitary figure.

'What the hell are they doing?' he muttered as they

pecked about the grass. Then he saw they were each carrying something in their beak and dropping it before flying off. Soon they were all lined up on the opposite roof again. Bob stepped onto the grass to see what they'd left there. It was a mixture of old bits of wood, stone and plastic and it took him a second before he realized they weren't just strewn about randomly.

'Bloody Nora!' he blurted out as he read the words 'DUN ADD' quite clearly on the grass.

His gull flew down and landed gently by the garden spade which was leaning on the back wall. This was another first.

'DUN ADD? What the bloody hell does DUN ADD mean?' The bird pecked at the spade. 'What?' said Bob picking it up. 'Do you want me to dig for worms?' The gull flew off at that, leaving Bob holding the shovel in his hand. 'I'll need to check this out on the Internet,' he said putting the spade down by the fence and going in to switch on his PC.

'Jesus!'

Dun Add turned out to be an Iron Age hill fort in Argyll. He could see from his bedroom window that the gull was still perched opposite. 'Sixty miles to Kilmartin – should be able to get there and back OK today.' He looked at his watch – it was 8.30. 'Nothing to stop here for – it'll be a nice day out.'

He returned to the back step and softly said, 'On my way.'

The gull flew down and landed on the spade by the fence.

'I get the impression you want me to take this,' said Bob picking it up. 'I'll put it in the boot.'

The bird flew off into the distance and was soon lost to view.

Dun Add was the site of the crowning place of the kings of Dalriada – the ancient kings of Scotland. So it said in the leaflet Bob took from the visitor centre. This was an 'Historic Scotland' site – not a place you go digging up at your leisure. The spade had remained in the boot of his car.

As he looked over at it in the car park he was amazed to see a gull sitting atop it. Surely it wasn't? But as he drew closer he saw it was his early morning friend.

'What the hell are you doing here?'

As it flew off he started up the engine and followed it. It stuck to the main road at first but five miles on it landed by a heavily wooded area. Bob pulled over by the trees and got out of the car. The bird was sitting on the boot.

'You want the spade? OK – we'll get it.'

Having retrieved the shovel he walked behind the gull as it led him further into the woods. After twenty minutes they came out into a glade where the sun shone brightly down. His avian companion stopped at the far end of it and pecked at the grass.

'I can take a hint,' said Bob, hurtling the spade into the earth, 'though I think this must be the craziest thing I've ever heard of.'

He was soon sweating – and wishing he'd brought some

water from the car – but he carried on and had soon dug quite a respectable hole in the ground.

I'd make a grand gravedigger, he thought as he pierced the soil again – but this time there was a clunk instead of a thud. 'Hope it's not bloody bones.' He carefully cleaned away the earth and saw it was anything but bones – it was …

'Buried treasure!'

A cache of golden artefacts lay revealed before him, all bearing the intricate decoration of Celtic design. The jacket he had recently thrown to the ground was hastily filled and tied together in a makeshift sack. As he turned to thank his feathered friend he was shocked to discover he was being watched by a tall, red-haired, bearded man dressed in animal skins.

'I am Fiadach, son of Eathach,' he said by way of explanation. 'King of Dalriada.'

'I'm Bob Graham – presently unemployed,' Bob replied.

The King of Dalriada smiled and stretched his arms above his head. 'You have broken the spell,' he grinned.

'Spell? What spell?' Bob asked.

'Come, sit by me and I will tell my tale,' said Fiadach. 'You would have made a mighty warrior in the days of Dalriada.' Bob said nothing – not entirely sure that would have been the case. 'You have strength, intelligence, boldness …'

'Were you the gull?' Bob asked by way of something to cover his embarrassment.

Fiadach looked into his eyes. 'For 2000 years I have flown.'

'Why?'

'A woman's jealousy.'

'Seems a bit harsh,' said Bob.

'The Veiled One is a harsh mistress.'

'The Veiled One?'

'Listen to my tale, my brother,' said Fiadach softly. 'Once I ruled over all you see,' he began, sweeping his hand around the landscape. 'All men feared me in battle and respected me in the Great Hall. For a queen I chose Anu, the fairest of the fair, and our love was a bond that could never be broken. One day, as I hunted in these very woods, Cailleach Bheur – the Veiled One, Goddess of Winter – came to me, prinked and preened with languorous eye, swelling breast and lascivious smile – but I had already fallen into love's snare, and gladly, with Anu. The temptress could not sway me and grew angry as I spoke of she whom I loved so well. The more I rejected her, the angrier she became until finally her fickle, vain and cruel ways broke loose and she screamed in her vexed frustration …'

'A King you are, a King you'll be,
King of the Gulls who haunt the sea.
Return a man through food from one
From winter moon to summer sun.'

'And thus I became the King of the Gulls. Nor did I see any hope of change. For only when one person had fed me from Midwinter Day to Midsummer Day would I be free of the spell. For 2000 years I have roamed the skies – until you carried out the instruction the Veiled One had laid down.'

'Glad to be of help,' said Bob. 'What will you do now?'

'You have been my saviour. I can never repay what you have given me – but this world is not mine.'

'Thank you for the gold,' said Bob.

'It is as nothing to what you have returned to me. But now I must go – my people await me,' he concluded and raising his hands to his mouth he gave three great cries of 'AUK! AUK! AUK!' which floated out on the summer breeze leaving silence between the two men – but not for long, as soon a host of gulls appeared, swirling down to grasp their king and carry him far into the sky.

'Farewell!' he cried and Bob watched as he grew smaller and smaller until he finally disappeared to his new home.

Bob's journey home was uneventful but when he phoned Scottish Heritage they were more than happy to meet him when he explained what he had found with his metal detector and, although it took some time, the £2.5 million he eventually received for his treasure trove made unemployment just that little bit more bearable.

THE WRITER

I

AT twenty-three I was a failure. I felt it keenly. Only a year before and the world had been my oyster. I had, after all, just graduated with a first class honours degree in English Literature and had a keen vision of a life spent researching amidst piles of musty tomes. A year to the day later here I was, checking the next day's Daily Gazette crossword clues for spelling errors. And so, I reiterate – I was a failure.

In the months following my graduation I had despatched my CV to countless literary establishments thinking I would be able to take my pick of the crop of offers that would be winging their way through my letterbox. As time went by and the 'We regret to inform you' replies mounted daily, my rose-tinted ambitions began to mist over in direct correlation to the depletion of my bank balance. Finally, as my desperation grew, I saw I would have to aim lower, take anything I could get in fact, simply to keep the wolf from my door. A clerical vacancy at the Daily Gazette was advertised; I applied and was successful in obtaining the post – and six months later I was a failure.

'Right folks, listen up,' said Gerald, our overtly gay office manager, clapping his hands to get our attention. 'A little bird's just told me The Guvnor himself is going to be making his annual foray into our neck of the woods this afternoon, so I want everyone to be on their toes with head down and arse up – figuratively speaking – because Sir Trevor's one of the old school with a fine regard for the Victorian work ethic and he doesn't suffer fools gladly. You all know the script – he'll stroll in, talk to me for two minutes and then bugger off for another year. Just make sure you all look the part for those two minutes. Any questions?'

There were none. With the exception of me everyone in the office had been there for a number of years. They took the news of the imminent arrival of their illustrious employer, media mogul Sir Trevor Sullivan, with a collective sigh of concern and then continued going about their business. I glanced at the clock on the wall and saw it was five minutes past my lunch break. Ninety seconds later I was reading my book in the cafe across the street. It was reassuring to know I could still act with alacrity when the need arose.

II

When I got back to the office I saw a tall, distinguished looking man deep in conversation with Gerald in his office; it was obviously Sir Trevor. Having hastily dumped my book on the desk I took off my coat and settled down to look as busy as the rest of my co-workers. No sooner had I started than I heard Gerald's door open followed by the quick step of expensive shoes growing louder behind me as they drew nearer. The two minutes were up for this year and all we had to do was wait a few more seconds when he would once again become 'He who must be obeyed' up in the clouds of what we called 'The Penthouse Suite'. As the sound of shoe leather on tile reached its peak – it suddenly ceased. I could feel the tension in the air around me; this was unknown territory.

'Are you reading this?' Sir Trevor asked as he picked up my book.

As I turned to face him I was tempted by the ironic reply that I was using it as a coaster but I settled for the simpler, 'Yes.'

'Know anything about him?'

Having written my English Literature thesis on the author in question I once again felt able to reply in the affirmative.

His deep blue eyes bored into mine. 'What's your name?'

'Fiona,' I replied.

'Fiona?' he mused. There was a slight pause then, 'My office – ten minutes.'

With that he was gone.

'Did I hear right?' gushed Gerald rushing up the aisle. 'Did Sir Trevor just invite you to his office?'

'No Gerald – he ordered me to his office.'

'Oh my God! I've worked here for ten years and I've never seen his office!'

'Would you like me to take some pictures?'

Such was his excitement that the sarcasm went completely over his head.

'What did he say?'

'He asked me my name and if I was reading this book.' I held it up for Gerald's attention.

'Oh my God! Not again!'

'What?' I enquired, somewhat taken aback by his response.

'Nothing – you'd better get up there. Take the lift to the 18th floor.' Suddenly he hugged me. 'And good luck.'

As I walked through the office with all eyes upon me I realized how the condemned prisoner on Death Row feels as he takes that final, fateful journey.

III

The 18th floor was much posher than the one I worked on. Sir Trevor's immaculately dressed and perfectly coiffured PA pointed to a door without uttering a word. I found myself sitting in a high-backed chair facing my employer across a desk the size of no man's Land.

'Patrick Bellamy,' he said, 'what do you know about him?'

I reamed off a screed of facts until Sir Trevor was satisfied I was a veritable cornucopia of knowledge on the subject. He held up his hand and I stopped in mid-sentence.

'Do you know where he's living now?' he said.

'Presumably still in Kilcraggan – he's been there for over forty years as far as I'm aware.'

'I want you to go there.'

'What!'

'I want you to go there and interview him.'

I laughed out loud. 'He hasn't given an interview since 1963!'

'Nevertheless – I want you to go there. Do you drive?'

'Just about.'

'Good. Get an early shuttle up to Glasgow. We'll arrange for a hire car to be waiting for you.'

'When?'

'What's today?'

'Wednesday.'

'Friday then – that'll give you tomorrow to research – take the day off – I'll square it with Gerald. I'll send Anne down with the tickets later.'

This was obviously my cue to depart, but I remained firmly seated.

'Well?' he said.

I shook my head.

'It's an opportunity, is it not, young lady?'

'It is,' I admitted.

'Think of the furore if you manage to pull it off.'

'Scores have already tried – and failed.'

'Including three from here,' said Sir Trevor, 'but none had your knowledge – or beauty.' I believe I blushed. 'What do you have to lose?'

He was right – at worst I'd be back checking crossword

clues next week. A rush of adrenalin surged through me as I rose and extended my hand to shake his.

'I'll give it my best shot, sir.'

'That's all I ask, Fiona – that's all anyone can ask. Leave your mobile number at the desk with Anne in case I need to contact you.'

IV

Thursday was a free day. I didn't need to do any research. I'd been there, done that and bought the proverbial T-shirt when I wrote my thesis. I was excited – but not in the way I expected to be. How many times had I imagined this happening? It was my fantasy daydream – an interview with Patrick Bellamy.

Yet something was nagging at me; my bubble was certainly at full expansion – but I had a feeling I wanted to burst it myself. Was it just nerves? Or was it the fact that facts were in short supply where Patrick Bellamy was concerned?

He was the archetypal Man of Mystery. Born in Macau in 1923 to a Scottish mother and an Irish father; orphaned at sixteen; fought in the Ardennes campaign in World War Two; wrote six novels between 1947 and 1955; refused to accept the Nobel Prize for Literature in 1959; was sentenced to two years in prison for wounding his lover with a handgun in 1960; bought a croft near Kilcraggan in 1963 – and hadn't been heard of since.

Kilcraggan, in the heart of the Scottish highlands, was in the middle of nowhere. Bellamy's croft, being some three miles from the village, could rightly be described as being in the middle of nowhere in the middle of nowhere. There was no electricity and just a hand pump for water. It was life in the Dark Ages – and at eighty-six years of age Bellamy was surely nearing the end of it. That last thought was enough to bolster me. If he was ever going to talk then it would surely be now, with his span well beyond the allotted threescore years and ten.

I could have re-read the two slim biographies that had appeared during his lifetime, but neither were worthy of the name. There was barely enough known about Bellamy to fill a pamphlet never mind a book. My thesis 'Sexual obsession in the novels of Patrick Bellamy' had, fortunately, required me only to examine the characters forged in the writer's imagination and not the man himself – though it appeared obvious to me the co-relation was a strong one.

V

Did I mention it was November – and freezing? I had been planning for an overnight stay in a quiet, picturesque Scottish hotel in the Highlands but my hopes were soon dashed when I received the plane tickets. I was on the first flight from London to Glasgow and the last flight back.

Friday was a cold, raw morning. I'd booked a taxi for 5 a.m. and was up, quite literally, in the middle of the night getting everything ready for its arrival. A bowl of cereal and a cup of coffee was all I could manage before it drew up, bang on time I must say, on my doorstep. The flight was at

7 a.m. and after booking in at Heathrow I grabbed a sandwich and another coffee before boarding. Everything went very smoothly and by nine o'clock I was driving my hire car out of Glasgow Airport and pointing it in, what I believed to be, the right direction. I'd printed off a route map from an Internet site and I was happy to see a sign for Greenock – that proved I was on the right road.

By the time I reached Loch Lomond it was starting to rain, a sleety rain that made the wipers screech as they traversed the windshield. At one point I thought about stopping at a cafe for some lunch but I had bought some bits and pieces at the airport with a can of juice so I decided to pull into a lay-by and have a hurried snack.

By now it was 11.30 and I was close to Glencoe. The sheer scale of the scenic beauty stunned me. Another forty-five minutes found me near Fort William. I took a right, as per my printed instructions, and it wasn't long before I saw the sign for Kilcraggan.

If there was a Twilight Zone then this was surely it. The village consisted of five houses, a shop come post office and a pub. I drew up in a space alongside the pub, The Friar's Breeks it was called, and quickly made my way inside, as the rain was falling heavily by now. Two men, the only inhabitants, who were sitting at the bar, looked up from their pints with surprise writ large upon their faces. A head appeared from a door behind the bar and all three gave me the once over.

'Is it the Fort William road you'll be looking for?' said the man behind the bar.

'No – it's Kilcraggan I'm looking for.'

'Well you've sure enough found it,' he replied with a broad smile.

'I'm looking for Patrick Bellamy's croft.'

His mouth opened slightly and his head moved a little to the left.

'Mr Bellamy is it?'

'Yes – do you know where it is?'

He picked up a cloth and began to clean a glass. 'He's a private man is Mr Bellamy.'

'I know,' I replied.

'Doesn't take too kindly to being... disturbed.'

'I know that too.'

'There's been others came to visit who got short shrift as I've heard.'

'I appreciate your concern but I'd still be obliged if you could point me in the right direction.'

'Ah well,' he smiled, 'it's no business of mine – and there's no law against pointing a young lady in the right direction. Just follow the road here and take the second opening on your left – you'll find Mr Bellamy's place soon enough.'

'Thanks,' I said and then as a realization stuck me I added, 'Do you think I might use your toilet? I'll be happy to buy a soft drink.'

'No need for that – there's no 'customer use only' policy here – we're all customers in Kilcraggan. First door on your right.'

Having relieved the pressure in my bladder and freshened myself up a little I felt more able to face the world.

'Thanks again,' I said as I walked past the bar.

'Happy to oblige you miss. Remember – the second opening on the left – and an opening is all it is mind – it's not what you could call a road.'

'I'll take care,' I said.

'You take extra care, miss,' he said with a strong emphasis. 'Especially when you reach the croft.'

I smiled ambiguously and walked out.

VI

He wasn't joking when he said it wasn't what you could call a road. I stopped by the track for a full two minutes wondering if I'd make it through the mud – and, more importantly, make it back again. Finally I took my courage in both hands and began edging forward. It was a track for a four-wheel drive vehicle, bumpy and muddy with the rain but after a mile it broadened out a bit and progress became somewhat smoother.

At last I saw a little whitewashed cottage with smoke coming out of its chimney. I stopped beside a wooden gate some fifty yards from the house and got out of the car. The smoke I took to be a good sign – at least he was at home – but then again, he was always at home apparently.

The grass was long, wet and muddy and I hadn't taken it into consideration when I'd pulled on my shoes that morning. The walk to the door of the croft was a torturous one – but I made it at last – soaked to the skin and with feet squelching. As I stood there in the doorway I looked around me; there was nothing but a vast wilderness in all directions. Grasping the knocker I gave the door three hard raps and stood listening to the wind howling through the glen. Nothing. I rapped again – still nothing. Walking round to the window I tried to peep through the dirt of years. I could see the fire burning in the grate and thought I recognized a human figure sitting nearby, possibly reading a book, but there was so much grime it was impossible to be sure. I gave the window a good rattle and shouted 'Hello?' Still nothing. I rattled the window again. 'Hello?' Nothing. I moved back to the front door and renewed my acquaintance with the knocker. 'Hello?'

'Bugger off!' came a querulous voice from within.

'Mr Bellamy?'

'Bugger off!'

'I'd appreciate it if you could spare me a few minutes.'

'Bugger off!!'

'I won't take up much of your time.'

'What part of bugger off don't you understand?' The voice that said that was just behind the door.

'I'd like to ask you a few questions.'

'Is it English you don't understand?'

'I've come a long way.'

'Is that my bloody problem?' The door burst open. 'What age are you?'

'Twenty-three,' I replied, taken aback by the sudden sight of this ancient, lined visage with its shock of unruly white hair.

'Well I'm eighty-six – so I've come a damn sight bloody

longer way than you, wouldn't you say?' I was too shell shocked to say anything. 'Who sent you?' he asked.

'The Daily Gazette.'

'That bloody rag!' he snarled. 'They sent someone a couple of years ago – a little shirtlifter.'

'Shirtlifter?'

'Poofter, bum-boy, arse pirate, faggot …'

My mind went back to Gerald's hug. 'I think I catch your homophobic drift. Does it make any difference if I say I'm not a lesbian?'

'Different thing altogether,' he replied.

'Different? In what way?'

'Women understand women – that's why they're so good at hating each other. Men don't understand men – or women.'

'So you give your tacit approval to female homosexuality but not the male variety?'

His piercing blue eyes looked me up and down as if I was a lost dog.

'Jesus – you're in some bloody state,' he said shaking his head. 'You'd better come in and dry out by the fire.'

VII

A wave of euphoria swept over me but I kept it bottled up with a simple, 'Thank you.'

It was certainly a male domicile – a mess. There was one room and a small kitchen. The fire was a godsend. I felt its heat hit me as I walked through the door.

'Give me your coat,' he said. I was happy to oblige. He took it and put it over the back of a wooden chair which he moved closer to the fire. 'Shoes.' I took them off and he rubbed off the worst of the mud with some old newspaper pages before placing them on the chair. I sat down then gave an involuntary leap as he knelt before me and began drying off my feet with a towel. 'Never had a foot massage?' he leered.

'It was rather – unexpected.' The feeling wasn't unpleasant.

'Put them up here,' he said, pulling over a wooden box for the purpose. I did as he asked and felt the fire warming my soles and toes. He took a half-full glass of whisky from a nearby table and quaffed it down before pouring out another one and offering it to me.

'This'll heat you up inside.'

'I'm driving.'

'Bugger driving – drink it – or you're out on your arse right now.'

I took the glass, closed my eyes and swallowed. The heat on my feet was nothing to the heat it caused as it went down and settled in my stomach. I caught my breath and gasped.

'I usually drink Pimm's,' I wheezed by way of explanation.

A disapproving grunt was his only response as he settled down into a decrepit armchair facing me – bringing the whisky bottle with him. He took the glass from my hand, refilled it for himself and lit a cigarette.

'Smoke?' he asked.

'No thanks.'

'You're no bloody fun at all,' he rapped. 'Are you one of these modern women I used to read about?'

'Must be – maybe I'll grow out of it – in time.'

'True,' he mused, 'you're young yet. Life's got a few kicks up the arse put by for you I'm sure.'

I reached into my handbag and drew out my minidisc recorder with its small microphone.

'Do you mind if I record our conversation?' I asked.

'Who said anything about having a conversation?'

'I thought that's what we were doing.'

He shrugged his shoulders – which I took to be a sign of his grudging approval.

'It's a hell of a small tape recorder,' he said.

'It's a minidisc.'

'Minidisc?'

'Part of the modern world us modern women inhabit.'

'Wasn't the world modern when they were laying King Tut away in the Valley of the Kings?'

'I suppose it's all relative. He poured more whisky into another glass and handed it to me. 'I'm driving!' I protested.

'You're driving nowhere – look,' he said pointing to the window where heavy snow could now be seen falling.

'Christ! I'm supposed to get the last shuttle back to London.'

'Tomorrow's another day,' he smiled.

'I can't stay here!'

'You were keen enough to get in a few minutes ago!'

'But –'

'Scared by the tales of my libido?' he asked with a sly grin. 'Don't worry – those days are gone.'

Perhaps the alcohol was making me bold. 'And do you miss those days?' I asked.

He laughed. 'Jesus! That's quite a question to ask – when I don't even know your bloody name.'

'It's Fiona.'

'Is it now?'

'Fiona Bellamy.'

One eyebrow shot up. 'You're not my bastard love-child come to claim your inheritance are you?'

'Mere coincidence – though it was your name that first attracted me to your work.'

'Work? Is that what you call it?'

'What would you call it?'

'Scribble, scribble, scribble – that's all it is. Miners work; bricklayers work – writers scribble, scribble, scribble.'

'Why did you stop scribbling and come here?' I asked.

'I had nothing left to scribble. To use the miners analogy again – the seam had run out.'

'I did my final year thesis on you.'

'Well there's a bloody waste of time and effort if ever I heard of one,' he chuckled. 'And what conclusion did you reach?'

'That you were sexually obsessed.'

He roared with laughter. 'It took you a year to find out that a man was sexually obsessed? You should have pulled in the nearest bar and saved yourself the trouble.'

'Are you implying all men are sexually obsessed?'

He leaned over and put his hands on my knees as he stared into my eyes. 'Show me a man between seventeen and seventy-one who isn't – and I'll show you a corpse.'

'Do you get many visitors here?' I said hastily.

He sat back in his chair and sighed. 'People come – like you.'

'And you send them away?'

'Yes.'

'Don't you get lonely?'

'Lonely?' he questioned. 'We're all bloody lonely.'

'But it's so – out of the way here.'

'That's why I chose it.'

'How do you fill your days?'

'With walking – and this,' he said holding up his glass, 'and this' – his cigarette, 'and that' – an antique transistor radio, 'and those' – a bookcase in the corner.

'Mind if I take a look?'

'Be my guest.'

I paused by the table to pick up a copy of Montaigne's Essays. The bookcase contained mainly classics – Ovid, Seneca, Homer's Odyssey, Plutarch's Lives and Essays. There were a few poetry anthologies and The Complete Sherlock Holmes.

'Is Conan Doyle as modern as it gets?'

'Anything that had to be said was written well before the Huns sacked Rome,' he replied.

'None of your own works?'

'They're lying around – somewhere.'

'Were the classical authors a big influence on you?'

'I hadn't read any of them before I came here.'

'Is it an age brings wisdom thing?'

'Age?' he barked. 'Age brings dementia, arthritis, brittle bones – anything but wisdom.'

I picked out a well-thumbed copy of the love poems of Catullus from a shelf. 'Do you like Catullus?'

'He was a fool – albeit with a fine turn of phrase.'

'It's been well read.'

'Fools consort with fools – and he understood the torture.'

'Of love?'

'Of love – and hate.'

'You shot the woman you loved.'

'Christ!' he shouted, becoming animated. 'It was only a flesh wound in the shoulder – a nick for which I spent two years in the nick at Her Majesty's Pleasure!'

'Yet you still say you loved her?'

'Of course I love her – I wouldn't have shot her otherwise! Do you seriously think I'd go around shooting just anyone?'

I was formulating an answer when he rose from his chair still talking. 'Although here's what you get for killing four strangers.'

He went into a drawer and took out a small box which he threw over to me. I opened it to find a white enamelled cross with a blue and red ribbon.

'Distinguished Service Order – in case you don't know,' he said returning to his seat. 'Funny old world, eh? Kill four strangers and they give you that. Nick the arm of the woman you would die for and they put you away for two years. Explain that one to me?'

'You killed four men?' I said softly.

'It was either that or they would have killed me.'

'During the war of course.'

'Christmas Day 1944 in the Ardennes.'

'Wasn't that the Battle of the Bulge? I thought only American troops were involved in that.'

'Oh it was a Yank thing true enough – but there were a few Brits there – Special Ops stuff.'

'You could only have been –'

'Twenty-one? Yes, barely old enough to shave – but it's nothing new – and it's still going on today – there'll always be a war somewhere.'

He lifted the glass to his lips moodily.

'Can we talk about your … scribbles?' I asked.

'I don't know that I've got much to say about them.'

'I've been re-reading Lewd Minx.'

'Wasn't once enough?'

'Othello isn't it?'

'Damn her – lewd minx,' he quoted, 'O damn her!'

And so it began. For the next two hours I asked and he answered. I think he was genuinely impressed by my knowledge.

'You know more about it than I bloody well do,' he said. 'Maybe I should be asking the questions.'

It began to grow dark and he fetched in two old paraffin lamps. As he began lighting them my mobile phone blasted into life and he almost knocked one over.

'Jesus! What the hell is that racket?'

'My mobile – someone's sent me a text,' I said reaching into my bag.

'Mobile?'

'Mobile phone.'

He took it from me and looked at it in amazement – which quickly turned to horror. 'You mean there's no peace? They can find you anywhere – even here?'

'That's the modern world.'

'Well it can go and screw itself,' he replied quietly, tossing it back to me. The message turned out to be nothing more exciting than my service provider telling me I'd get free weekend texts if I topped up with £20.

'What do you do for food up here?' I asked.

'The girl from the post office brings me stuff up on the last Saturday of the month. Are you hungry?'

'Starving.'

'Well – she's due tomorrow – but I'm sure there's enough left for a couple of fry-ups – unless you're watching your weight.'

'I am,' I replied. 'I'm trying to increase it.'

He turned to the black, Victorian range with a laugh and it wasn't long before bacon was sizzling, eggs were frying and sausages were spitting.

'Fried bread?' he asked.

'Yes please.'

'Tattie scone?'

'Mmm!'

'There – that'll put some fat on your bones,' he

announced, handing me a plate with enough on it to feed a famished family of four.

'HP?' he asked.

'To die for!' I replied, splashing on the sauce.

'Tea or coffee?'

'Tea please – milk, one sugar.'

'Right you are, ma'am,' he said with a wry glance.

We settled down to eat in silence for a few minutes. The room looked cosy with the lamps and the fire burning in the grate. I began to think there might be something to the idea of living a life of isolation – but maybe that was the whisky, which had certainly mellowed me out.

'I mentioned earlier you loved Claire – but you came back with the present tense.'

'You don't stop loving someone just because they're dead,' he said. 'I'll always love Claire.'

'I can't understand how you can hurt someone you love.'

He stopped with his fork halfway to his mouth and looked at me. 'Then you've obviously never been in love,' he replied.

My mind drifted to the two semi-serious relationships I'd had in my life. 'I don't think I want to be – if that's what it leads to.'

'You can't say you've lived if you haven't loved.'

'Is that the old, 'Better to have loved and lost than never to have loved at all' bit?'

'Or as Tennyson said, 'Better to have loved and lost than never to have lost at all',' he answered.

'Isn't that like saying a woman's never lived if she hasn't had a child?'

'Any woman can have a child – that's got nothing to do with love.'

He poured out some more tea from the pot for himself.

'Do you regret refusing the Nobel Prize?' I asked.

'Not at all – I set a trend,' he grinned.

'You mean Sartre?'

'Yes – and I agree with what he said.'

'What was that?'

'I thought you were literary minded?'

'I don't know much about Sartre – except that he was ugly and talked about the bourgeoisie a lot.'

'I've never read a word he wrote – but I liked his style when he said, 'A writer must refuse to allow himself to be transformed into an institution – even if it takes place in the most honourable form'.'

Another couple of hours flew by. It was intoxicating simply listening to him speak. I tried to focus on the fact that he was eighty-six years old – he should have been shuffling around, taking his medication, having a carer come in to pat him on the head saying, 'And how are we today my love? I'm Rose – remember?' Instead he was a Titan with total recall – or so it seemed to me. His fingers, deep brown with nicotine, punctured the air as he made his points. His passion was that of a young idealist. I realised I was glad I'd never met him in his prime, as it might have ended up with him looking down a gun barrel.

'Right,' he said at last, finishing off the last of the whisky, 'bedtime. I'll kip in the kitchen – you can have the bed settee.' He pulled the chair beneath him and it rolled out on the floor. 'My only mod con.' My protests were in vain. 'You'll need the heat – my old bones are used to the cold up here – one night won't kill me.'

'Is there a toilet?'

'Toilet? Of course there's a toilet,' he laughed. 'Here you are,' he said, handing me a chamber pot. 'Just empty it out the back door when you're done. I don't want you walking to the septic tank tonight.'

He turned and wrote a few words on a piece of paper. 'And here – take these,' he said handing me three large notebooks.

'What are they?' I asked.

'My journals. I've occasionally jotted a few thoughts down during my time here. Here's a note saying I'm giving them to you – just in case of any future problems.'

'But – but – what'll I do with them?' I stammered.

He shrugged his shoulders. 'Wipe your arse? Light the fire? Write the biography?' He extended his hand to me. 'I'll say goodbye now – I get up early and go walking for a couple of hours each morning.'

'I don't know how to...' I began, shaking his hand.

'Then don't!' he interrupted. 'Just live your life, Fiona – and enjoy what you can of it. Looks like there's a thaw on,' he said looking out the window on his way to the kitchen. 'I think you'll be OK getting out in the morning – but take care.'

VII

I slept fitfully, yet when I woke and checked my watch it was 9 a.m. The kitchen door was slightly ajar – I remembered it being tightly closed before. He had obviously wakened early and gone out walking as he said he would.

My ablutions were rapid. All I wanted now was to get home – to start reading the journals which were lying on the table beside me with his letter.

There had indeed been a thaw – my feet got wet and muddy again – but the track was passable and I was soon on the main road heading in the direction of Glasgow Airport.

It was 5.30 p.m. by the time I touched down at Heathrow and almost 7 o'clock when I threw myself into my familiar armchair at home. I had eaten only a ham and cheese sandwich all day and was in the process of preparing a quick microwave meal when my mobile rang.

'Hello.'

'Fiona?'

'Yes?'

'It's Trevor.'

Trevor? Trevor who? I thought. 'Oh – Sir Trevor? Hi, I'm …'

'Sorry to send you on a wild goose chase, my dear.'

'What?'

'All that way and no chance of anything.'

'Sorry?'

'No – it's I who am sorry. Daresay you've seen the papers.'

'Papers?'

'Apparently he had been lying dead for over two weeks – the girl who delivered food to him once a month found him this morning – she had a key to get in. I can only imagine what state she must be in. Take a few days off Fiona – must have been a trial for you – going all that way to find a locked door and no one answering. I'll square it with Gerald. Bye.'

He rang off before I could say anything.

I whirled my head round and saw the journals and the letter lying on my chair with the minidisc on top of them. I snatched the recorder up and plugged my headphones in as I pressed play. My voice came through immediately, I suppose it's all relative … silence, then I'm driving! … silence … Christ, I'm supposed to get the last shuttle back to London … silence … I can't stay here! …silence …

The hairs on the back of my neck rose as my stomach fell to the centre of the earth. I grabbed for the note he had written:

'To whom it may concern. I, Patrick Bellamy, have given my journals freely to Fiona Bellamy' – his signature was unmistakable. I reached for the notebooks – they were solid. As I leafed through them a calmness descended upon me – every page was full of scribble, scribble, scribble.

A CHANGE OF CAREER

I

I worked as a clerk for solicitors Erskine, Stangoe & Towner. The hours were long, the pay was poor and the work was arduous. When they told me they were downsizing and would be replacing me with a computer program I shook them each by the hand and thanked them. I don't think I had ever felt so happy in my life.

The month following my enforced dismissal was a halcyon one. I rose when I pleased, ate when I pleased, read when I pleased and went to the pub when I pleased. It was an insight into Paradise. All that changed when my bank statement dropped through the letterbox. Doing as one pleased was an expensive business. With a groan of resignation I realised I would have to rejoin the rat race.

I was thirty-six years old, unmarried with no children I was aware of. I entered the local Jobcentre with a high degree of expectation and was soon sitting at a desk explaining my all too obvious reason for being there to my designated client advisor. A barrage of questions followed and my heart began to sink under the weight of paperwork I was being handed to fill out. Not content with what he had supplied me, my nemesis rose to obtain some other sixty-four page booklet which required my immediate attention. I was in the act of heaving a sigh such as only the recently unemployed can when my ears became attuned to a squabble which was developing at the desk next to me.

'But that's not what I want!'

'It's the way things –'

'This is a Jobcentre, is it not?'

'Yes but –'

'People come here seeking employment presumably?'

'Yes, but we –'

'Look, young man. I've already explained my position. I've not come here looking for employment but looking to employ someone. Can you or can you not supply me with information that will lead to my request becoming a reality?'

'There are rules you have to follow, sir. You can't just –'

'Rules! Don't talk to me about following rules – I was in the RAF for thirty-five years!'

'If you'll just go through the proper channels I'm sure –'

'Damned waste of time coming here. Country's gone to the dogs.'

He certainly had the look and bearing of a military man, grey bushy moustache and all. His eyes suddenly fell on me.

'You sir.' I pointed to myself. 'Yes, you sir. Are you here seeking employment?'

'Yes,' I answered.

'Are you literate?'

'I believe so.'

'Numeric skills up to scratch?'

'My mother taught me my times tables.'

'No bad habits? No skeletons in the cupboard?'

'Not that I'm aware of.'

'Then the thing's settled – the job's yours, sir!' He rose and shook my hand with such a firm grip I winced. 'Here's my card – call on me tomorrow after ten. You see how easily a thing is settled between gentlemen?' he said to the hapless civil servant he had been arguing with, then turning on his heel he was gone. My client advisor returned a minute later to find I had done the same.

II

To cut a long story short, Wing Commander Robert Nuttal (rtd.) had decided to write his memoirs and was in need of a Personal Assistant. The hours were short, the pay was excellent and the work was minimal.

I would drive to his Victorian villa each morning, record his reminiscences into a Dictaphone, asking questions and seeking clarification on points here and there, leave about 2 p.m. and then go home and turn his rambling monologue into readable form on my word processor. He was delighted.

At the end of two months we had covered the greater part of his military career and I'd heard a host of yarns from his time in Aden, Egypt, Cyprus, Pakistan and the Persian Gulf. He was a colourful character and the book was full of entertaining anecdotes. We had high hopes it would find a publisher.

One morning I arrived as usual and, after tea and some polite conversation, we settled down to the work at hand.

'Not sure if I should include this, Atkinson,' he began. 'Bit of a rum tale – but I'll let you be the judge.'

'Sounds interesting already,' I said.

'Oh it's interesting enough – but perhaps not the sort of thing for a military memoir.'

'Is there a skeleton in your cupboard?' I smiled.

'Enough skeletons to fill every damn coat in the cupboard – but this is an entirely different thing,' he replied.

'I'm getting more intrigued by the minute.'

He lit a cigarette and fingered it nervously.

'In December 1980 I was sent to RAF Woodbridge in Sussex. It was an American base and my remit was to liaise with the base commander regarding any threat the Russians might pose – you have to remember it was still very much a Cold War scenario then. At about 4 a.m. on Boxing Day I was awakened by an outbreak of activity on the base – lots of noise and running about. I dressed quickly and went to see what all the fuss was. The chap in charge, name of Conrad, was initially very unwilling to disclose any details of what was going on – and I soon discovered why when he eventually told me there was a UFO incident taking place.'

'A UFO!' I exclaimed.

'Of course I laughed out loud at the idea – you know what these Yanks are like – seen too many B-feature science fiction films – 'Klaatu barada nikto' and all that. As we stood there a sergeant burst in – looked as if he'd seen a ghost – started gibbering about strange lights, a craft of unknown origin and being given a message in binary code by aliens! He'd made some notes and showed them to us, also a drawing of the craft – it was in Rendlesham forest. Of course I was of the opinion he was delusional but Conrad sat him down then turning to me asked if I'd like to accompany him to the scene of the close encounter. Having nothing better to do I agreed to go with him.'

I was on the edge of my seat. 'Did you see the spaceship?' I asked.

'Didn't see a damn thing. We spoke to a few other chaps who confirmed the sergeant's story about strange lights – but not the craft itself. They also said that livestock on an adjacent farm had been making a hell of a racket – as if they were in a state of panic and terror. Conrad had a lamp and we set about examining the area with the aid of that and a Geiger counter.'

'Any radiation?'

'Nothing out of the ordinary, but we did find three triangular burn marks and some broken branches on the trees near them. There wasn't much more we could do in the dark so we secured the area and returned to the base, debriefed the sergeant and prepared to wait until it grew light in the morning.'

'Did the sergeant have anything to add?' I enquired.

'He was very shaken – and he wasn't a man to jump at shadows. I'd seen him tear strips off several of the privates during my stay. That's what struck me as being so strange. It was obvious he had suffered some kind of trauma – but it seemed impossible to believe his tale of an extra-terrestrial craft. Perhaps I should rephrase that – as during the debrief he told us the occupants had informed him, via telepathy, as he never actually saw them – that the binary code message was to inform us that the craft was from Earth's distant future, that they meant no harm and were there to collect genetic material to save the future human race which was near extinction during their era. So in effect they weren't extra-terrestrials – they were terrestrials from the future – time travellers if you like.'

'What an incredible story!' I said.

'Yes – incredible is the word,' Nuttal replied with eyebrows raised.

'Did you find anything when you returned to the forest that morning?'

'By that time we'd had word from the meteorology people that abnormally low lying cloud and the pulses from a nearby lighthouse reflecting on it was in all probability responsible for the strange lighting effects that were reported. The broken branches were put down to foresters who had been working in the area.'

'That doesn't explain what the sergeant saw.'

'No – nor the triangular scorch marks on the grass. To answer your question – we did go out and scout around – but we didn't seriously believe we were looking for evidence of a spaceship.'

'So you found nothing else?'

'I came across a patch of green, gelatinous material – took a sample of it – but it was deemed to be some kind of lichen or frog spawn or something of the sort. Forests are full of gooey green stuff.'

'What happened to that?' I asked.

'I kept it,' Nuttal replied.

'Kept it?'

'Yes, as a souvenir.'

'Where is it now?'

'Must be lying about here somewhere. I scooped it up using an empty cigarette packet at the time – haven't given it a thought since to be perfectly honest.'

'I'd love to have seen it.'

'Then so you shall, Atkinson – so you shall,' Nuttal replied rising from his chair. 'Pour us both a brandy and I'll see what I can do to assuage your curiosity.'

At the end of half an hour I was starting to feel guilty about sending him on a wild goose chase when he came through the door with the packet in his hand.

'Damnedest thing, Atkinson,' he said.

'What?' I asked.

'Well you'd expect it to have dried up after thirty years in the dark of a desk drawer, but look –'

He flipped the cigarette packet lid back to reveal exactly what he had described to me – a green, gelatinous gooey material.

'Good Lord!' I exclaimed. 'That's a strange one. Don't suppose you have a microscope?'

''Fraid not old boy.'

'Would you mind if I borrowed it? I've got an old Victorian one – purely ornamental as far as I'm concerned but I'm sure it would do the job.'

'Be my guest,' he replied handing it over. 'May as well

keep it – I've no use for it. But what about this whole episode – do you think it should be included in the book?'

I replied very positively in the affirmative.

III

Victorian artefacts were built to last. I was careful to avoid any contact with the gel as I smeared some on to the glass slide of the microscope – possibly because I had seen too many sci-fi films where such contact turns one into a creature from the black lagoon. But of course it wasn't as if I really expected to see anything unusual through the lens.

I had some difficulty focusing at first but then the sample came into view with crystal clarity – and I saw that it was throbbing. I drew my head back with a start and then tentatively took another look. It was indeed quite definitely throbbing – there was a steady pulse every second or so. But what did that mean? Certain lichens can live dormant for millennia. A closer examination revealed a hexagonal cell-like structure to the gel, but was it cells I was seeing? I was no scientist. Interesting all the same.

I poured myself a drink and began to look for information on the Rendlesham UFO on the Internet – there was plenty of it – and conspiracy theories abounded. Nuttal was mentioned several times but always in a bridesmaid and never the bride kind of way – a peripheral figure who wasn't connected to the main event. Of course I knew differently.

I'm not entirely sure what happened next. I'd imagine

the combination of long day, exciting story, late night and whisky combined to lull me gently to sleep in my chair. I don't know how long I was out. That's the thing about sleep – have you been out for ten seconds or ten hours? It's impossible to tell when you come to initially.

My first thought was that the house was on fire – a thick haze of smoke enveloped me ... but it couldn't be due to fire as it was a chilly smoke, more akin to fog. My laptop was still switched on and a succession of zeros and ones were flying across the screen at great speed. I tried to move and realised I couldn't – apart from my eyes. What they saw was a trail of green gel going from the microscope to the cigarette packet and from there ... into the USB input of my computer!

I felt a presence behind me – but couldn't turn. I was absolutely terrified. I think they sensed that because they quite suddenly came in view. I could see it was a male and a female – the general shape was there. They were hairless, their eyes were larger than normal human eyes but the mouth, nose and ears had all but disappeared. The male addressed me not in words, but telepathically.

'Do not be alarmed.' His voice was robotic, yet calming. 'We mean you no harm.' For whatever reason I truly did believe him. 'We come from Earth's future and require genetic material to save our race – your race as it will be.' He paused as if awaiting a response. I saw that he was an amalgam of both the carbon based human and the silicon based computer. Somewhere in the future they had become one. 'You will feel no pain,' he went on. The woman held something to my hand – that was the last thing I remember.

When I came round the fog had gone, as had the green gel. There was a price to pay though – my laptop hasn't worked since. When I took it to the repair shop the guy said he'd never seen anything like it. 'It's as if every circuit has packed its bags and left!' Thank goodness I had backed up Nuttal's book on a disc.

So – that's the story of how I saved the world God knows how many years in the future. I was hoping to add that to my CV for my next Jobcentre interview but it wasn't necessary. Nuttal, to whom I mentioned nothing of the above by the way, was so impressed by my work that he got me a job with one of his friends at the Ministry of Defence. I've been there five years now and love every minute of it. Lots of free foreign travel involved too.

As for Nuttal's book – it turned out to be a great success and has already gone through three editions – though I wouldn't put it past the old codger to be buying up all the copies himself!

GENTLEMEN OF THE ROAD

FROM a philosophical viewpoint I had always been in the camp of Democritus rather than Heraclitus – that is laughing at the stupidity of life rather than weeping over it. The Spartan notion of feeling sorrow when a child was born into this vale of tears and celebrating when someone was fortunate enough to depart it also struck a sympathetic chord in my psyche as I grew older. Life seemed to me to be a series of minor and major inconveniences, with the odd carrot of joy thrown in as an afterthought, a token gesture from the unconcerned Fates as they weaved their tangled webs.

My own death was a fairly typical one, a heart attack in the local bookmakers. It's ironic that it occurred at one of those carrot moments I spoke of – I had just watched the horse I had bet on romp home in front at odds of 25/1. Sadly I was unable to collect my winnings.

I found myself drifting through a foggy landscape but after a time it cleared to reveal I was standing on a seemingly endless road. On my right I saw a baby sitting on the grass amidst a pile of old clothes and, coming towards me, were two young men wearing ill-fitting suits that I would have expected to see on their respective grandfathers. They walked in a dilatory fashion, their features expressionless and listless.

'Where is this place?' I asked.

'Are you a new arrival?' one of them replied.

'Presumably so,' I said. 'Where am I?'

'No one knows,' his companion answered.

'What?'

'No one knows,' he reiterated tonelessly.

'I'm afraid you've lost me,' I said.

The first, a fair-haired, pale skinned man gave a wan excuse of a smile.

'We are all lost here,' he said.

'Look,' I said, 'I'm trying to find out exactly where I am and where I'm supposed to go.'

'Go anywhere,' he said.

'Anywhere,' his bespectacled companion added.

'Am I dead?' I asked.

'Yes, we all are.'

'John Davies,' I said, holding out my hand – to no response.

'Touching is not permitted,' said the one with the glasses. 'My name is Daniel Peacock.'

'And I am William Hardy,' said his accomplice.

'Can either of you tell me anything?' I asked.

'We died – like you,' said William, 'and found ourselves here.'

'But where exactly is here?'

'No one knows,' said Daniel.

'What do you do here?'

'We walk,' said William.

'We walk the road,' Daniel intoned funereally.

'That's all very well – but where does it lead to?'

'No one knows,' said William.

'Do you know anything?' I asked in some frustration.

They looked at each other – was it surprise I caught a glimpse of?

'We know we grow younger,' said William.

'Younger?'

'We grow younger,' William repeated.

'What? Each day?'

'There is no day,' said William.

'There is no night,' said Daniel. 'There is simply this,' he cast his hand around him, 'and the road.'

'But how do you … live? Is there food? Shelter?'

'There is no food – no shelter,' said William. 'No one eats; no one sleeps. There is no sun, no moon. There is no touching; there are no emotions; no love, no hate. We walk the road and grow younger – like him,' he concluded, pointing to the baby by the wayside. 'Soon his time will be over and he will go.'

'Go where?' I asked.

'No one knows,' said Daniel. 'It is like death on Earth – no one knows whence we go.'

I made to grab him by the shoulder but was rebuffed by what seemed to be magnetic repulsion.

'There is no touching,' he said in the same monosyllabic tone.

'How long have you been here?' I asked.

'I was seventy-eight when I died,' the young man replied.

'Good God!'

'My time will come – as will yours. Perhaps this is purgatory – a waiting place where we can discuss our past life free of all emotions and prepare for whatever is next.'

'It sounds more like Hell!' I exclaimed. They looked at each other again. 'I think I'd rather kill myself than live like this.'

'Touching is not permitted,' said Daniel, raising his hand to his face where I saw it was repelled just as my own had been. But that wasn't the case as far as I was concerned – as I realised I was scratching my chin!

'You should not be here,' said William. 'You have shown emotion – and touching …'

'… Is not permitted,' I said with a grimace. 'Yes – so you said. But how the hell can I get …' A thought came to me and I pulled a pocket knife from my jacket.

'This, gentlemen, will either work – or it won't. Thank you for your time and I wish you luck – wherever you end up.'

With that I plunged the blade into my heart.

'Clear!'

An electric shock ran through my body and I convulsed into consciousness.

'I've got a pulse! We've got him back!'

My eyes blinked open to reveal a paramedic putting an oxygen mask on my face.

'Let's get him out of here – we're not home yet,' he said.

That was four years ago and I'm now as fully recovered as one can be from cardiac arrest. The conversation with

William and Daniel was not a dream to me – it was as real as the book you are holding in your hand. I believe that, like Scrooge, I have been given a chance, whether by accident or design, to change things – and change things I have. I still believe my philosophy to have its foundation in fact, but I now appreciate that life might not be quite the demon I previously thought. There is after all roast beef, warm sunshine, malt whisky, music, laughter with friends and the love of a good woman.

I intend to make the most of it – and in becoming one of lives givers, not takers, I hope to avoid walking on that never ending road when the hour of my death finally strikes.

THE CHILD

I

CHARLES GRAHAM drew the line at jogging, but he was in favour of taking at least a little exercise and could be seen walking his well-worn route each morning after breakfast; down Farm Road, past the old Wheeler place, up as far as the water treatment plant and back down again via West Street. At a steady pace it took him forty-five minutes.

The Wheeler place had been boarded up since ever he could remember, so it was quite a surprise when he passed it one bright Tuesday morning in March to find the boards were all off the windows and the front door was lying open. Just at that moment a young woman holding a camera came through the said door and began snapping away at the exterior of the building. Charles was curious enough to strike up a conversation.

'Excuse me,' he said, 'has the house finally been sold?'

The woman turned around. She was about thirty-five, with shoulder length blonde hair and an interesting rather than beautiful face.

'Yes,' she replied. 'I've bought it.'

'It's been up for sale so long I'm surprised the estate agents didn't give you a fiver to get it off their books.'

She laughed and walked across the overgrown front lawn to greet him.

'Amanda Martin,' she said holding out her hand.

'Charles Graham – pleased to meet you. You've got your work cut out here.'

'It's certainly going to be a challenge to get it back to its former glory. Are you local?'

'Yes,' Charles replied. I live just up the road there – Derwent Way.'

'Do you know anything about the house?'

'Only that it's been up for sale since Noah built the ark. I believe there was a fire in the 1960s – Mrs Wheeler was rescued but died later in hospital.'

'Was that the previous owner?'

'Yes – before my time though. There are a couple of prospective centenarians in the pub who would no doubt be able to tell you more.'

'Do you know them?'

'Oh yes. Bob and Alec are there every night between seven and nine. You can set your watch by them. Do you have plans to live here when it's restored?'

'Yes – I've always wanted a place in the country.'

'I'm not sure if this could be termed the country.'

'It is for a city girl like me,' she said. 'I've been based in London for years as a freelance photographer.'

'Where are you living in the meantime?' asked Charles.

'I've rented a flat in town – Berwick Street.'

'I know it well.'

'I'm going to do a before and after article on the house – hence the camera.'

'You'll need a few workmen in before the after part.'

'Daddy's going to take care of that,' she smiled, 'as my birthday present.'

'Good old daddy', thought Charles as he continued on his way.

II

Amanda – or her father perhaps – wasn't one for letting the grass grow under her feet. Each day as Charles passed by he observed a time-lapse scenario as the renovations continued apace. Skips appeared and were quickly filled and despatched; new windows and doors were put in place. By the end of two months he hardly recognized the place. During that time he had never seen the new owner but one fine morning in May – as the folk song goes – there was Amanda, getting down and dirty with a multitude of weeds in the front garden.

'Hello again,' he said. 'That's quite a turnaround in the old place.'

'Isn't it,' she beamed. 'I've been whizzing around Europe on various photo shoots, then I had to tie up things in London, so I only got back yesterday – and I'm amazed at how much progress there's been.'

'Your father must have a hex over the great British workman – you'll have to find out his secret and let me know.'

'I'd imagine he simply waves bundles of fifty pound notes in front of them,' she laughed. 'He thinks money solves every problem.'

'He's not far wrong – but it's not everyone who has access to that kind of incentive.'

'Daddy's very generous – but he's really hopeless with money.'

'It's fortunate he appears to have so much of it then. Are you still in Berwick Street at present?'

'Yes, but once the bedrooms here are finished I'll be able to move in.'

'I see you're not afraid of getting your hands dirty,' Charles said, nodding to the spade she held.

'Daddy brought us up to believe that one must work hard – even if one is rich. I find it's always very fulfilling to do manual labour.'

'I wonder if the navvies who built the railways would share your philosophy?'

Amanda laughed. 'I do take your point – I have the choice while they didn't. What line are you in?'

'The retired line.'

'Gosh! You look much too young to be retired.'

'Shouldn't that be the man's line?' Charles returned. 'I'm afraid I'm much older than I appear to be – I've lived a sedate life.'

'What age are you – if you don't mind my asking?'

'Forty-six.'

'Retired at forty-six!'

'Retired at forty-four. I had built up a hi-tech company

and sold it to the Yanks. Sadly I don't have your father's work ethic and I'm quite happy to potter about in a nondescript sort of way nowadays.'

'Sounds ideal,' said Amanda.

'It suits me very well,' said Charles. 'But if you'd like any help with the house – or garden – I'll be happy to put my hands to the pumps. Keeping the flab at bay by walking every morning gets a bit tedious.'

'That's very generous of you – tomorrow shall we say?'

Charles laughed. 'I've done it now, but I'd hate to see your hands covered in blisters while mine stay lily white. Tomorrow then. Ten o'clock?'

'Ten o'clock – and be sure to wear old clothes.'

'No problem there,' said Charles, 'all my clothes are old.'

III

Next morning found Charles digging alone in the summer sunshine. Amanda had gone indoors to upload her photographs of the house onto her laptop computer.

'Charles?' she suddenly called.

'Yes?'

'Could you come in a minute please?'

Charles was only too glad to pitch his spade in the earth for a while. It was all a bit much like hard work and the blisters he had joked of were fast becoming a reality.

'What's up?' he asked as he joined her.

'Look at this,' she said, turning the computer so he could see.

'What?' he asked.

'There,' she said, pointing to an upstairs window on the photo on the screen.

'Yes – it's definitely a window,' he said.

'But there –' she went on. 'I'll zoom in.'

As she did so Charles saw what she was talking about.

'Good Lord!'

'So you can see it too?'

'Must be a trick of the light – a reflection on the glass.'

'A reflection that looks like a child?' she said.

'Well it can't be anything else – unless you think it's a ghost.'

They both peered at the screen and the fuzzy outline of what appeared to be a child's face.

'Boy or girl?' Amanda asked.

'I couldn't say – well, of course I can say – it's neither – it's just a trick of the light.'

'It's a bit weird – eerie. He looks rather angry.'

'So you've decided it's a boy?' said Charles.

'I suppose I have.'

'What shall we call him? I'm thinking he's Edwardian – how about Cedric?'

'Stop pulling my leg!' Amanda laughed. 'You're just an old cynic.'

'Well I've never been one for believing in ghosts.'

'What about mediums?'

'What about them?'

'Don't you believe they talk to spirits? I went to a medium once – quite a scary experience.'

'But all they seem to do is say your aunt Nellie is here

and she misses you. They never seem to impart information of any worth. You would think if they've made the effort to break through the ether they could at least tell you the winning lottery numbers for the following week.'

'Didn't you tell me about two old men who went to the pub each night?'

'Bob and Alec?'

'Yes – that's them. I believe I'll have a word with them tonight. They might be able to shed some light on things.'

'I'm sure they'll know more of the house's history than anyone else around here.'

'Would you care to join me?' Amanda asked.

'I'll be glad to,' Charles replied, 'As long as you get your round in.'

IV

'Them Wheelers was bloody strange folks,' said Bob.

'Ladies present,' said Alec.

'Beg pardon, miss,' said Bob, in what was almost a ritualistic call and response.

'In what way were they strange?' Amanda enquired.

'There was goings on up there.'

'Young Beth was in with a racy crowd,' Alec interjected.

'Beth who?' asked Charles.

'Beth Wheeler of course!' said Alec, amazed that his statement could have been in any way misunderstood.

'She were an 'andsome woman,' the irascible Bob put in with a leery grin.

''Andsome is as 'andsome does,' said Alec. 'Her ma and pa didn't like it much.'

'Could we start at the beginning please?' said Amanda. The two old men eyed her grumpily. 'When did the Wheelers move into the house?'

'Some time between the wars – they was there when I were a nipper – I was born in 1925,' said Alec. 'Beth were a young woman by then – twenty years old maybe.'

'Beth was the Wheeler's daughter,' said Bob by way of explanation. 'She were one of 'em bright young things – flippers.'

'Flappers?' said Charles.

'That's what I said, didn't I!' snapped Bob. 'Yeah, she was a flapper – 'ad all the young men in a bloody flap alright!' He gave a throaty chuckle.

'Ladies present.'

'Beg pardon, miss.'

'They was a warm lot,' said Alec.

'Who were?' said Amanda.

'Her friends – there was parties when her ma and pa weren't there.'

'Arty types,' said Bob, giving Charles a conspiratorial wink.

'Is Beth the Miss Wheeler who was in the house when it caught fire?' asked Amanda.

'The same – Beth never left that 'ouse. Seemed to be that summat happened. I seen 'er father go grey almost overnight – and 'er mother died not long after,' said Bob.

'Beth lived with her father till he died. When d'ye reckon that would that be, Bob?' Alec asked.

'Just after the war – 1947 or 48. Then she lived there till the fire took 'er.'

'When was that?' asked Charles.

'Couldn't say for sure – it was late in the 60s.'

'Did Beth have any children?' Amanda asked.

'No – weren't no kids – she never married. Never left the 'ouse after her pa died.'

'Do you have any idea what caused her father's hair to turn white?'

'No,' said Alec. 'They kept themselves to themselves. Funny you should mention kids though.'

'Why?' asked Charles.

'Just what Beth was saying when they brought 'er out of the 'ouse when it was on fire. Raised a few eyebrows – but she'd been pretty doolally for years by then by all accounts – and then the smoke and all …'

'What did she say?' Amanda asked.

Bob sank his pint, placed the empty glass on the table and wiped his mouth with the back of his hand. 'She were saying it was the child.'

'The child? That caused the fire?'

'I dunno about that – all I know is that folks told me she kept repeating it over and over – it was the child.'

'I'll get a round in,' said Amanda.

The old men's eyes brightened.

'You could do worse than go and 'ave a talk with Nancy,' said Bob.

His friend heaped scorn on the suggestion. 'Nancy's as doolally as Beth was.'

'Who's Nancy?' said Charles.

'Nancy Brown. She were 'ousemaid to the Wheelers,' said Bob.

'She's in cloud cuckoo land now,' said Alec. 'She's got that Alkaheimers.'

Charles didn't correct him. 'But she's still alive?' he said.

'Yes – she's still alive – if you can call it living,' said Alec. 'She's in that home in Cranston.'

V

Late next evening Charles's phone rang. It was unusual for him to get a call so late.

'Hello?'

'Charles!' It was Amanda – in a very emotional state. 'Oh Charles! Can you please come over? Please say you'll come. I'm –' The line went dead.

Throwing on his coat Charles rushed down the road as fast as his legs would carry him. He felt instinctively that it was the Wheelers and not Berwick Street he should make for.

When he got there the place was in darkness. Amanda was standing outside the door.

'Amanda!'

She threw herself sobbing into his arms. 'Oh thank God! Thank God you came!' she cried, shaking hysterically.

'Ssh … ssh …' he said calmly as he caressed her hair. 'It's OK. Ssh …'

'Oh please take me away from here – take me away … but don't leave me!' she sobbed frantically.

'Come on – let's go. Take my arm – nothing's going to harm you.'

As he turned to move off up the front path, out of the corner of his eye he caught the briefest glimpse of a figure in the upstairs window. The malevolence he registered caused the hairs on the back of his neck to rise and a juddering tidal wave of horror to all but overwhelm his nervous system.

'What's wrong?' cried Amanda.

'It's nothing,' said Charles recovering his composure. 'Just the chill.'

By fits and starts he managed to get Amanda into his flat where, after drinking a mug of hot, sugary tea, her shivering finally ceased.

'What happened to you?' he asked.

Her saucer-like eyes seemed to widen even further.

'I saw him, Charles!'

'The boy?'

'He made sure I saw him.'

'Where did you see him?'

'I was washing up in the kitchen when I simply knew someone was behind me. I looked in the window facing me and saw his reflection in the glass. When I turned round he just stood there, almost daring me to approach him.'

'Did he approach you?'

'No,' said Amanda. He just stood there for about a minute – he had such a cast to his features – a brutal, sullen malignancy verging on the demonic, Charles! I was almost scared out of my wits! Finally he melted away and I was able to call you – but then of course the phone cut out.'

Charles made up a bed for his unexpected visitor and poured them both a generous whisky.

'Here,' he said 'Drink this – it'll help you sleep.'

'Thanks,' she replied taking the glass.

'What will you do with the house?' Charles asked.

'I don't know – but I don't want to set foot in it again. Maybe Daddy will think of something.'

'I'd like to try speaking to Nancy,' said Charles.

'The maid?'

'Yes.'

'Didn't old Alec say she's got Alzheimer's?'

'Yes – but I'd still like to try. She must know something if she was there during that period.'

'Would you mind if I went too? I'd rather not be left alone at present.'

'Of course,' said Charles. 'I was rather hoping you'd accompany me.'

'Tomorrow then?'

'Yes, tomorrow.'

VI

'I'm afraid you won't get much out of her,' said the nurse. 'She rarely speaks – she's ninety-seven now,' she added, as if to explain the patient's lack of communication.

They sat down on either side of the old woman in the

wheelchair who was staring out of the large bay window which looked onto the back lawn.

'Nancy?' said Charles – to no response. 'We've come to ask you a few questions.'

Still the frail figure gazed vacantly out at the grass.

'We've come to ask about Miss Wheeler, Nancy,' said Amanda – but still Nancy's impenetrable gaze remained unmoved. 'Do you remember the Wheelers – and Beth? Do you remember Beth?'

Nothing.

'I think we're wasting our time,' said Charles. 'She's in a different zone from us.'

All at once Nancy's bony hand shot out and grabbed Amanda's.

'How's your husband now?' she asked. 'Is he still dead?'

'Yes … yes he is,' Amanda replied slowly, trying to feel her way into a conversation. 'And yours?'

'Oh yes,' smiled Nancy, 'Still dead.'

'And Beth?' Amanda offered.

Nancy frowned. 'Beth?'

'Beth Wheeler – you remember her, don't you?'

'Ah yes,' said Nancy with a chuckle. 'I remember Beth – she's dead too – all dead – all them Wheelers – all dead – Francis too.'

'Francis?' said Amanda.

'Dead,' the old woman repeated, rocking to and fro in her chair. Suddenly she leaned forward and whispered in Amanda's ear. 'But no one's to know.'

'Of course not,' said Amanda. 'It's a secret.'

'Secret!' she smiled happily. 'Yes – it's a big secret.'

There was a moment's silence. Amanda was wondering how to move things forward when Nancy spoke again.

'She had to do it.'

'Had she?'

'Oh yes – it was him or her.'

'I see.'

'Seven years they kept him hid.'

'As long as that?'

'Oh yes – seven years. Didn't even know who the father was – she had so many young men you see.'

'Of course. But you knew the secret.'

'I was well paid to keep quiet,' Nancy whispered holding a finger to the side of her nose.

'Was he a good boy?' Charles asked.

The old woman's head spun round sharply to face his. Her face contorted with fury as she slowly spat out her reply.

'He – was – the – Devil!' Then the fury was gone, replaced by a forlorn sadness. 'She wouldn't even give him a name.'

'Francis?'

'Mr and Mrs gave him that. She just called him the child – always – even that last night.'

'What happened that night?' Amanda asked.

'It was the scream I heard.'

'Francis was screaming?'

'No – Beth – it were Beth. Me and the Mr and Mrs ran upstairs. Francis was lying on the floor – dead – stabbed to the heart – oh there was such a mess!'

'Good God!' Charles said quietly.

'Beth was saying, 'It was the child, He tried to kill me'.'

'She murdered her own child?' said Amanda.

'I believed her,' Nancy said in a whisper. 'She were bleeding herself from the knife. The child were evil – he could have murdered us all.'

'What happened to the child's body?' Amanda asked.

'Old Mr Wheeler built a new fireplace – that's where Francis went – that was a secret too. I didn't stay long after that – there was noises. Mr Wheeler gave me a lovely recommendation – and a nice bit of money too – and I got a position with a Lady,' Nancy smiled.

VII

'We believe it was an electrical fault, miss,' said the fireman as they stood in the ruins of Amanda's home. 'It's lucky you were out at the time.' He turned to answer a question from a colleague.

'While we were talking to Nancy your house was razed to the ground,' said Charles.

'It was the child,' Amanda said quietly. 'Excuse me,' she said to the firemen. 'Would it be possible for you to smash the fireplace?'

They looked at each other. 'Smash it?' said one.

'Yes,' said Amanda. 'I have reason to believe there's something hidden behind it.'

'A secret treasure chest?' the fireman grinned. 'OK lads – bring a couple of hammers over.'

They worked steadily for a few minutes and finally the edifice began to crumble.

'Watch out – a couple of more clouts will do it.'

At the third blow the fireplace collapsed into a pile of rubble – and sticking out of it was a human bone and a small skull.

'Jesus! What's that?' said one of the firemen.

'It's the child,' said Amanda.

THE MYTHS OF TIME

I

I was sitting in a bar with a man named Claude Varron. He was elderly, sallow faced, clean shaven and his watery grey eyes held a myriad of secrets. Although we were indoors a slushy snow lay under our feet and, here and there, the grass could be seen where it had melted sufficiently.

We were discussing the ways of Fate and the vicissitudes of Fortune. It seemed to us both to be a subject worthy of debate and, though our opinions differed on some points, there was no offence taken on either side; no raised voices; it was all very civilized.

'No man can escape his Fate,' said my companion. 'The lives of the unborn are already etched in stone. We are as puppets in the hands of the puppeteer; jerking marionettes who dance our pre-ordained dance with no hope of ever breaking free from the tangled strings which hold us – whether we be king, beggar or thief.'

All at once the bar grew dark and the background chatter vanished.

'That's a bit rum,' said Claude, which struck me as being amusing – given our location. Then I awoke.

Next day I answered a knock at my door to find two policemen standing on the front step.

'John Fairclough?' said one.

'Yes,' I replied.

'Might we come in for a moment and have a word with you?' said the other.

Who was I to refuse? I could think of no reason for their visit. I had no parents, children or relatives who might have died; my TV licence was paid and I was not in the habit of using either hard or recreational drugs.

The two men sat down. I offered them tea or coffee, but they declined.

'How can I help you?' I asked.

'Are you familiar with a man by the name of Claude Varron?' said the older of the two.

For a moment I couldn't place it – dreams vaporise so quickly.

'I don't think so,' I replied, just before the penny dropped – though it seemed astounding that they would be questioning me regarding a man who appeared in my dreams.

'The thing is,' the officer went on, 'he was found dead late last night – and the only item in his possession was a piece of paper with your address written on it.'

I did my best to hide my utter disbelief.

'Found dead you say? Where?'

'In a rented flat in Barnstow – he had just taken it yesterday.'

'Was he murdered?' I asked.

'It seems to have been a heart attack. A neighbour heard a cry and then a thump and alerted the authorities.'

'Surely there are some clues in his flat as to his history?'

'There's nothing, sir – all we have is the suit he was wearing – bearing the name of a London tailor in the 1950s – no longer trading … and this piece of paper.'

He handed it to me. My address was printed neatly upon it in blue biro.

'We have been making enquiries, but as yet we've been unable to discover anything as regards his background. We only know his name because he had to give it to the landlord. Does the number on the other side of the paper mean anything to you?'

I turned the slip of paper over to find 121 written there, this time in black ink.

'I'm afraid it means nothing at all to me,' I said.

The officers rose to depart.

'Well Mr Fairclough, if you should remember anything that you think might be of assistance to us please call me on this number, said the elder of the pair handing me a card.'

What could I do but mumble my acquiescence and close the door behind them?

II

I was atop a huge skyscraper on which a vast graveyard stood, stretching as far as the eye could see. I wandered through its expanse as one would wander through an endless desert – without hope. It seemed that all who had passed from earthly concerns were here interred for all eternity.

A pale moon glowed dimly in the starless sky; my legs grew leaden as I trudged on and on, into infinity; a dull inertia pervaded my very soul and I longed, ached, yearned – indeed I believe I begged for final release.

All at once I felt a hand upon my shoulder and I turned in abject weariness to find Claude Varron by my side. He said nothing, but gestured to the gravestone in front of us.

Claude Varron
1925–2012
Requiescat In Pace

'Where is mine?' I asked, as a child might enquire of a long sought after toy.

He looked at me impassively, but made no reply.

My eyes began to close as the intolerable weight of my exhaustion brought me to the brink of unconsciousness.

'No!' cried Claude, shaking me roughly.

I gave a start and felt a vibration go through my body; a wave that brought with it a return to life.

'There is something you must do,' he said.

'You're dead,' said I.

'The others deemed it was unnecessary for my body to continue,' he replied.

'Others? What others?'

His voice sank to a whisper. 'Who can tell?' I felt his

fear and saw that even the dead have dread. 'All we can do is obey.'

I wondered at what might happen to any who failed to follow this simple directive and found my mind invaded by a vision of what I can only describe as intense nothingness; a vacuum of stagnant emptiness, the horror of which brought me to the brink of the madness of Munch's Scream.

I knew it was a dream – no, a nightmare. I knew I was lying in bed, tossing and turning, bathed in sweat – but what good is knowledge to the subconscious elemental beast that wakes in us all each night as we sleep?

I saw I was defeated and resigned myself to the fact.

'What must I do?' I asked dully.

Claude seemed relieved at my question.

'There is a book you much purchase. It lies on the back shelf of the old antique shop in Stanforth High Street. It's title is 'Lost In The Myths Of Time'. You will buy the book and you will write out the first word of page one, the second word of page two, the third word of page three … and so on until you have completed every page. Do you understand?'

It all appeared childishly simple. 'Yes,' I said. 'I understand.'

At that the earth began to move under my feet and I saw I was on the edge of all things, gazing into an eternal black maw of emptiness. I grasped at its unspeakable blackness and clawed at its pitiless blankness and then, I fell, with Claude Varron's last words ringing in my ears.

'Accept your Fate …'

This time I didn't forget Claude when I awoke. I didn't forget any of it – I only wished to God I could.

I was like a washed out rag. My hair matted to my face with sweat, my heart racing in my chest. I showered and tried to shave, but gave up in the attempt as my hands were still trembling. All day I jumped at shadows. Even the sound of the morning paper coming through the letterbox caused a panic attack to assail me.

I confess that I had no wish to go to bed that night – the idea of sleep filled me with dread. But sleep I did, for who can fight it and win. Mercifully there was no repeat performance of the previous night's terrors. I awoke refreshed – and no wonder – I had been dead to the world for fourteen hours.

III

As the days passed my task began to weigh heavier upon me. I searched for the book online of course, but in vain. No mention was to be found of 'Lost In The Myths Of Time.'

Stanforth was fifty miles south. One dull day, late in November, I boarded the train that would take me there.

It was a little market town, filled with little market town people, rosy-cheeked plump young girls and hefty farmers' sons looking to waylay them. I wandered on down the cobbled High Street and soon found what I was seeking, 'Ye Olde Antique Shoppe', at number 121.

A bell above the door rang as I entered, but no one

approached. The only sign of life was a mug of coffee on the counter from which steam was rising. A sense of decay hung heavy in the air. Chipped jugs lay with tarnished copper ladles; distressed chairs hunched under ancient grimy tables. The flotsam and jetsam of those long departed lay hugger-mugger in disjointed heaps, each item with its own unknown history.

The decrepit bookcase at the back wall was my destination. My eyes scanned its shelves and almost immediately found their target. Surely only this timeworn, hidebound volume would fit in with the spirit of my nightmare dreamscapes?

I pulled it from the shelf and felt a shiver run through me as my hands made contact with the cover – for it was like no leather I had ever handled. Perhaps if I mention crocodile skin it would give some impression of its scaly form, but again, I felt remnants of hair upon it and something more than reptilian in the horror that it caused to creep upon me. One thing I knew for certain – no creature like this, if indeed creature it was, any longer walked upon this earth.

There was no marking on the spine but on the front I found writ in large gold letters, The King In Yellow. I felt that to open the volume would be madness – yet some force within me urged me to it and, much against my will, I let the pages turn at random and my eyes to fall upon them thus also.

Camilla: You sir should unmask.
Stranger: Indeed?
Camilla: Indeed it's time. We have all laid aside disguise but you.
Stranger: I wear no mask.
Camilla: [terrified aside to Cassilda] No mask? No mask!

With every sinew in my body at breaking point, I slammed the book shut and hurriedly thrust it back in place. My breathing was rapid, my heartbeat racing. I closed my eyes and stood there until my fear gradually diminished, feeling instinctively that had I read one more word I would have been driven hopelessly insane.

When I opened my eyes at last, they rested on 'Lost In The Myths Of Time'. It was no ancient tome, but a modern book for children. The colourful dust wrapper gave its title, amidst a painting of the enigmatic statues of Easter Island in the Pacific Ocean, and the author's name – Claude Varron. The year of printing was 1962. The publisher, The Saffron Press. I turned the first page and read the words I found there with amazement.

Dedicated to John Fairclough
– who made it all possible.

IV

Having returned home, with trembling hands I immediately set about noting down the cypher and soon these words, acting as fire upon brimstone, fell from my dry and parched lips.

> 'In ancient worlds they yet may live, those Gods whom time has thrown aside and cast asunder. Beyond the realms of man they dwell, obsolete exiles in a strange land, forsaken and forgotten in eternity. Time counts them dead, those old ones whom the past has buried, but Death is a stranger in that foreign land and, like the phoenix rising from the ashes of its own dissolution, they too shall yet rise from their ancient banishment to return in triumph to take that which is their due. Behold! For now I see the casting of the runes before me, as high above the lightning cracks to guide them on their way'.

And as I stood a bright, near blinding light burst forth from deep within the skies. Ten thousand trumpets blew, ten thousand drums were beat; I saw the seas rise up as if commanded by a force unknown to man, and in their wake I then beheld of countless millions, some afoot, some sat atop strange beasts, a sea of souls that saw an end at last to their eternal march which started long before the dawn of time; and at their head, his saffron robe bejewelled by all the stars, the King, unmasked – returned to claim his throne …

HAZEL

I

BRADSHAW was drunk, that much was obvious. The song 'Wide-Eyed and Legless' sprang to mind. I was wide-eyed myself, as I'd known him for forty years and had never seen a drop of alcohol pass his lips. I dragged him through my door and propped him up in an armchair. Black coffee was obviously required so I set about making some.

To find Bradshaw at my door in such a state was akin to finding the Pope in a brothel – not an impossibility, but certainly long odds against. I was unable to conceive of a set of circumstances which could have caused it to happen.

I forced a cup of coffee upon him and ordered him to drink it – which he did. At no point had he said a word so far. Taking the cup from him I put it on the table.

'Right, Bradshaw,' I said firmly. 'What the hell is this all about?'

His eyes became saucers in his balding head and he opened his mouth to speak, but only an incoherent, slurred mumble appeared. He tried to stand but I pushed him back. He tried again and once more I pushed him down into the chair. Finally he grabbed at my shirt, looked me full in the face and whispered, 'Hazel.' With that he promptly fell into a comatose slumber. I recognized the name – I should do – I was married to her for twenty years. So why, you'll be asking, is my friend so upset about her? Well, I'll give you a brief synopsis while he's in Dreamland.

Bradshaw, Hazel and I had all become friends when we were students at university. It didn't take long before we men felt more than friendship for this beautiful, intelligent, talented young woman. We were both in love with her – but she chose me. Bradshaw bit on the bullet and we all three always remained close – but he never did marry. Hazel and I agreed not to have children as we were more interested in our careers and that was that for fifteen years – until she vanished.

We hadn't rowed, we very rarely did and then it was usually my fault, nothing untoward was happening; it was, to all intents and purposes, just another Friday. Hazel went to catch the morning train; I took the car to the office; I came home at six – and she didn't. We found out she had been at work so must have disappeared after leaving it. At first I thought it was a simple case of her missing her train, but as the evening wore on I began to make some phone calls – though not to Hazel – she saw mobiles as an invasion of privacy. Finally I called the police.

It all becomes a bit hazy after that. Of course I was deemed the prime suspect in the case, but they couldn't find a trace of evidence – because there was none. Bradshaw was a rock, though I know for a fact he was every bit as upset as myself – and he too was questioned closely by the authorities. We clung on together during those first few weeks – but that was five years ago now.

I knew for a certainty that Hazel would never have left me in such a fashion. It was obvious she had either been the victim of a terrible accident – or murdered, the latter being much the more likely possibility. The lack of closure made it all the worse. I grieved without a point of focus, as did Bradshaw – who having slept for two hours was finally coming round. For a moment he was all groans, then he frowned, wondering where he was – then he remembered.

'I saw her!' he cried, bursting into life. 'I saw her Fairfax! Just as I'm seeing you now!'

I was taken aback by his words but tried to hide my emotions.

'OK – OK – calm down and you can tell me all about it.'

'She was on the train!'

'Your train?'

'No!' he said with a snort of disgust at my misunderstanding. 'The one on the other platform.'

'Slow down, Bradshaw, and let's take it one step at a time. You think you saw Hazel?'

'I know I saw her!' he exclaimed, thumping the armrest with his fist.

'Tonight, at the station?'

'I was sitting in my usual carriage on the 5.25 at platform three. On platform four, there was the 5.22 to Elderbrook – it's always the same.'

'I know.'

'Well, it started to pull out and I just happened to glance across at it – the train was still going very slowly – and she was there, Fairfax!'

'Did she recognize you?' I asked. The pause before he answered told me she didn't. 'How did she look?'

'Like … Hazel – just the same – but older, if you understand.'

'We're all a bit older,' I said. 'And you've never seen her on that train before?'

'For God's sake Fairfax – don't you think I'd have told you!'

I held up my hands. 'When you say she didn't recognize you – did you see anything in her features? Surprise? Shock?'

'There was nothing. She just looked at me for a moment then looked away – as one would look at a stranger on a train.'

I moved from the edge of the seat and leaned back in my chair. 'Did you tell the police?' I asked.

'No… I… I was so shaken I decided to steady my nerves and …'

'I know the rest,' I said.

'What should we do? Report it to them tomorrow?'

'I'd rather confirm it myself first.'

'But how can we?'

'Perhaps she's working.'

'What?'

'Maybe she's commuting – just like you and the others on those trains.'

'Do you think it's possible? Hazel working?'

'You say it was Hazel – and I've no reason to doubt you – but I'd like a chance to see for myself.'

'Of course.'

'If she is working then tomorrow, being Thursday, is a working day. What do you say I meet you when you leave the office and we'll see what we see?' Bradshaw nodded slowly. 'You'd best spend the night here I think.' Again he nodded slowly.

'Thanks,' he said. 'I think I'll go in a bit later tomorrow.'

'That's one of the perks of being the boss I suppose,' I replied.

II

'That's my train there,' said Bradshaw when we met next evening. 'Come on.'

'Wait!' I said, tugging him back. 'That's not the train we want – we need to be on the train you saw Hazel on.'

'Oh, right – then it's this one,' he replied, pointing to his left.

'Plenty of carriages on it,' I sighed.

'Plenty of commuters in London,' my companion replied.

'What time is it?'

'5.17 – why?'

'I want to wait until the last minute.'

'You'll be lucky to get a seat by then.'

'Where does it go – apart from Elderbrook?'

'I've no idea – best check the board.'

I walked to the end of the platform and saw there were four stops before the train reached its final destination. Just at that the guard's whistle blew.

'Fairfax!' Bradshaw shouted, jumping into the end carriage. I had to run, but I made it – just.

'No seats,' said Bradshaw looking around the compartment.

'We don't need them anyway – come on,' I replied, moving along the train. 'Let me know if you think you see Hazel.'

We began to edge our way slowly along the packed train with a succession of excuse me's, sorry's and my fault's. When we reached the fourth compartment, I stopped.

'What is it?' said Bradshaw earnestly. 'Have you seen her?'

I said nothing, but pointed to the back of a woman's head a few seats in front of where we stood.

'It's her!' Bradshaw whispered excitedly.

'Stay here – she'll recognize you from yesterday,' I said, indicating an empty seat I was going to make for which would enable me to see her face. She looked at me as I took my place – as fellow travellers do. There was no doubting that it was Hazel – and she didn't know me from Adam.

The train stopped soon afterwards and a few people got off, giving Bradshaw the chance to sit down. Ten minutes later, an announcement that the next stop was Berryton came through and Hazel began buttoning up her coat. Others too began making preparations for alighting there.

We watched as she stepped off the train and then followed her example. For a moment we lost her in the crowd but then Bradshaw pointed her out – she was heading for the nearby taxi rank.

'What do we do now?' he asked.

'Follow that cab,' I said, hurrying towards the next car.

'I've waited a long time to hear that line,' said the driver as we set off. 'You with MI5?'

'I'm afraid not,' I said.

'Private dicks?'

'I beg your pardon?' said Bradshaw.

'OK guv – ain't none of my business. As long as you got the readies I'll drive you from 'ere to Timbuktu – even if you're with the KG bleedin' B.'

It wasn't a long drive – five minutes at most. I asked the driver where we were.

'King Street, mate,' he replied.

'Number 48,' said Bradshaw, opening the cab door.

'No,' I said, putting a restraining hand on him.

'But she's in there, Fairfax!' he said angrily.

'Leave it – I don't want to shock her – or be shocked for that matter. We'll let the police know where she is and they can take it from there.'

'That bird give you a bit of grief did she?' the driver asked.

'You could say that,' I replied.

III

'It's definitely your wife, Mr Fairfax,' said Detective Inspector Maddox a week later. 'The DNA and the dental tests have both confirmed it beyond any doubt.'

'Does she know me?'

'She's been shown the missing person's report and read through the newspapers, but it all means nothing to her. She's been living under the name of Gillian Brady.'

'Has any explanation been forthcoming?' I asked.

'The white coats think it's most likely what they call a dissociative fugue.'

'Does that explain what she's been doing for the past six years? Her bank account was never accessed. How did she get the money to survive? What happened that evening when she left work?'

'I'm afraid she can't remember,' said the inspector apologetically. 'She's been working as a supply teacher for five years. We're still looking into various aspects of her disappearance. It's been quite a traumatic experience for her.'

'Traumatic for her?' I said.

'Well – for both of you obviously.'

I took a sip of the coffee he had provided. 'When will I be able to see her?'

'She's still in hospital at the moment, but as there doesn't appear to be anything physically wrong with her she'll be going home this afternoon.'

'Has she asked about me?'

'When she read the newspapers she asked if it was true she was married. When I said yes she replied, 'the poor man'. She seemed relieved that no children were involved.'

I gave an ironic laugh and rose from my chair. 'Can you tell me anything about her amnesia?' I asked.

'I've had the psychiatrist print off a fact sheet,' he replied handing me a piece of paper. 'You'll probably get more information on the Internet.'

'And it's OK to go and see her?'

He looked at me sadly. 'She's your wife, Mr Fairfax.'

IV

When I got home I read up on the dissociative fugue and found it was a rare psychiatric disorder, a psychogenic trance which caused amnesia of memory and individual personality, usually involving travel and the creation of a new identity. Apparently it happened to Agatha Christie for eleven days in 1926. One case study I read went on for twelve years! This certainly covered the facts in Hazel's case, but there was a hitch – the fugue was brought on by trauma or a stressful event. Neither had happened to Hazel – or had it? I began to doubt the very foundations of our fifteen year marriage.

I took Bradshaw with me that same night. I didn't want to leave it any longer – and I didn't want to see Hazel on my own.

She opened the door and looked at us as if we were insurance salesmen for a moment then –

'Oh!' – and her hand went to her mouth.

'Hello Hazel – sorry, Gillian,' I said quietly.

'You – you're David – my husband.'

'Yes – and this is our best friend, Bill Bradshaw.'

Her eyes moved from one to the other as if she was watching a game of table tennis.

'You'd better come in,' she said at last.

The living room wasn't Hazel at all – there was far too much clutter for her minimalist tastes.

'Can I get you something? Tea? Coffee?'

We both declined and sat down. Hazel clasped her hands around her knees.

'It's all rather … awkward,' she said with a fleeting nervous smile.

'So you don't recognize us at all?' I said. She shook her head and her lips tightened. 'You have no memory of us?'

Again she shook her head before saying, 'The doctors say I have some kind of amnesia disorder.'

'Do you remember leaving work that evening?' asked Bradshaw.

'No,' she replied. 'I can only recall going for an interview to be a teacher.'

'But that was a year after you disappeared!' I burst out.

'I know – but that's where my memory begins.'

'So you have no recollection of your childhood?' said Bradshaw.

'No – nothing.' She bit her lip nervously. 'I'm sorry for the pain it must have caused you both.'

Her eyes passed from Bradshaw to myself and – don't ask me why – it was then I knew.

'I think I'll have that cup of tea,' I said, rising and making for the kitchen. She made to get up but I forestalled her. It only took a second to lift a knife from the worktop and grab her from behind with the blade against her throat. A sharp hiss escaped her lips.

'Good God!' shouted Bradshaw, jumping to his feet. 'What the hell are you doing, man?'

'Who are you?' I whispered in her ear as I tightened my armlock. 'Where's my wife?'

Her breathing was rapid, beads of sweat were forming on her brow. I was expecting a physical reaction from her and my adrenalin was pumping, but after what seemed like an eternity she simply relaxed like a rag doll.

'Please, do not harm me,' she said – but in the voice of a man. 'Only the body of she whom you love will suffer.'

I slowly released my grip and moved the knife back from her neck. Bradshaw was standing like a statue.

'Who are you?' I repeated.

'It matters not,' she said calmly – nor would you understand.' Standing up slowly she turned to face me. 'The eyes are the windows of the soul,' she said, gazing into my own eyes, '–and that I could not hide from you. I must seek another host.'

With that her eyes rolled in her head and she collapsed back onto the settee. Her mouth opened and a thick fog began issuing from it – like ectoplasm, but vaporous. It rose slowly to the ceiling and disappeared. Her eyelids fluttered then opened. A puzzled frown was her initial response.

'David,' she said softly.

'Hazel!' I cried, hugging her to me. Bradshaw was quick to join us.

'Bill!' she exclaimed. 'What's wrong with both of you?'

At which we men laughed loud and long.

THE UNKNOWN SOLDIER

DETECTIVE INSPECTOR Ray Rowland mopped his brow as he made his way through the sunlit field. It was bloody hot. There seemed to be no end in sight to the heat wave. His sergeant, Alex Myres saw him coming and went to meet him.

'What have you got?' asked Rowland.

'Not sure, sir,' said Myres. 'Doc's looking at him now. Male, Caucasian, round about forty – naked.'

'Naked?'

'Well – it's the right weather for it,' said Myres.

'Any marks on the body?'

'None – dog walker found him – thought he was sunbathing at first.'

'No ID at all?' asked Rowland.

'Nothing – I've got them combing the area. Want to take a look?'

Rowland gave a grunt of assent and the two men walked up to the incident tent and stepped inside.

'Anything to report, Dr Shaw?' Rowland asked the bespectacled, middle-aged man leaning over the body.

'Ah! Inspector Rowland,' he said straightening up. 'Always a pleasure.'

'Likewise,' said the inspector with a forced smile. 'Any early indication of a cause of death?'

'Interestingly enough, yes,' the pathologist replied with a puzzled expression before sinking deep in thought.

Myres and Rowland looked at each other.

'And?' said Rowland.

'Hypothermia, old boy,' came the bemused reply.

'Hypothermia!' cried the inspector. 'It's eighty-five in the shade out there!'

'Interesting, what?' smiled Dr Shaw. 'It must make your day to have such a Sherlockian mystery thrust upon you.'

'What are you grinning at, Watson?' said Rowland sullenly, looking at his sergeant.

'Yes – there's no doubt it's hypothermia,' the doctor continued. 'I'll know more after the post mortem. Can't have been out in the open for more than an hour I shouldn't think.'

Rowland shook his head in amazement.

'Oh – there's one other thing,' said Dr Shaw as he peeled off his rubber gloves.

'Yes?'

'He has no fingerprints.'

'What? You mean they've been surgically removed?'

'No,' said the doctor closing his bag. 'I mean he's never had any.'

II

Early next morning Rowland and Myres were discussing the case – or rather the lack of one.

'So you found nothing?' said Rowland.

'Nothing at all, sir,' Myres replied.

'Anything from the house to house?'

'Nearest house is a mile off, sir.'

'So what we have is a naked man with no fingerprints who died of hypothermia on the hottest day of the year?'

'That's about the size of it, sir.'

The phone rang.

'Rowland,' barked the inspector, picking it up.

'Yes … Yes … What? Are you winding me up? We'll be right there.'

He slammed the phone down and looked up at his sergeant.

'Guess what?'

'What?'

'The naked rambler's gone walkies.'

III

Dr Shaw was understandably more animated than usual.

'It's just so incredible – impossible – the man was dead!'

'So what exactly happened?' said Rowland.

'I had him on the table – he'd been prepared. I went to get the paperwork relating to the case and when I got back – he was gone!'

'Is it possible he wasn't actually dead at all?' said Myres. 'Could he have been in some kind of deep freeze state – but still alive – and when he thawed out, as it were, he came back to life.'

'The man was dead, sergeant,' the pathologist replied – coldly.

'Dead men don't walk out of autopsy rooms,' said Rowland. 'Myres could have a point. Isn't that what cryogenics is all about – deep freezing the body?'

'Yes – the dead body, inspector!'

'But how did he get out?' asked the sergeant. 'Aren't all these doors electronically controlled? Don't you need a swipe card to get through them?'

Shaw and Rowland looked blankly at him for a moment before going to the door – which opened with a push.

'Get someone down here to look at these,' said Rowland. 'I want to know what happened here. Alert the airports, main railway stations, ports. I don't want this guy – whoever he is – leaving my patch.'

'Dr Shaw!' came a cry from the corridor as an intern rushed towards the three men. 'It's John!'

'What's happened?' asked the doctor.

'I found him upstairs, unconscious – someone's taken his clothes!'

IV

I know not who I am.
I know not where I am.
I know only my task.
My task is my reason for being.
It must be accomplished.
I must not fail.
Failure means death – for all.

V

'I spoke to John Davidson, sir,' said Myres. 'He didn't hear anything, didn't see anyone. One minute he was looking through a microscope – next he was waking up naked with us standing over him.'

'And the doors were all fused you say?'

'No one can tell us how – but yes – they've all been fused. The sparkys are all scratching their heads.'

Rowland shook his.

'None of this makes any bloody sense,' he muttered – as much to himself as to Myres.

'No sir – it does all seem to be a bit sci-fi.'

'Eh?'

'I said it's a bit like the plot of a science fiction film.'

Rowland grew thoughtful. 'Expand a little on that, Myres.'

The sergeant was taken aback.

'Well ... it's ...' he stuttered, '... like – there's a man in deep freeze in 3269 who's sent through time back to Earth to ... do whatever men who are sent back through time do, sir.'

'And such a man may well have no fingerprints,' said Rowland.

'Very likely, sir.'

'And he'd be able to ... confuse sparkys, one would imagine.'

'I suppose he would, sir.'

'Did you run his photo through the database?'

'Yes sir – no matches.'

'A man who doesn't exist,' said Rowland quietly.

'Yes sir – or at least, not yet.'

The inspector took a sip from his plastic coffee cup and frowned.

'I've got a bad feeling about this case, Myres,' he said.

VI

'He's arrived.'

'Intact?'

'It seems so – according to transmissions everything appears to be functioning normally.'

'Let's hope to God he remembers what he's supposed to be doing.'

'God?'

'Brush up on your history!'

'There's no way back for him, is there?'

'No,' the other replied quietly. 'The sacrifice is his – for the good of us all.'

'He'll become a legend – if we make it.'

'Like God,' laughed the other ironically, before ending with, 'He already is – to me.'

VII

'You and your guv'nor ever solve that frozen John Doe case?' asked Sergeant Owen.

'Nah,' Myres replied, handing his companion a cigarette.

'We couldn't get anywhere with it. Still nags at his brain though – mine too to be honest.'

'How long's it been now?'

'Over a year, why?'

'Just that I read something in the paper this morning that made me think of it.'

'What's that?' Myres enquired.

'It was about some bloke they found in the middle of nowhere at the North Pole – burned to death. Imagine – minus forty there and they find a barbeque. Made me think of yours – hypothermic in a heat wave.'

'You still got it?'

'Right here,' came the reply as Owen pulled the paper from his pocket. 'Page nine I think – wasn't much.'

VIII

'So – what do ye reckon, sir?' asked Myres.

'It's him,' said Rowland folding the newspaper he held in his hands. 'I can feel it's him.'

'Me too,' said Myres. 'Do you think he did what he had to?'

The inspector sipped at his coffee for a moment.

'I bloody well hope so, Myres,' he said. 'I bloody well hope so. To me he's the Unknown Soldier.'

HOTLINE TO HAPPINESS

ON reflection I, Sam Lawrence, found myself in a grey catchment area of arid wilderness, somewhere between life and boredom. It was a bad place to be – or so I thought at times – when I did think – which wasn't often. Not a lot happened; nothing changed. But already I'm lying, because change is as inevitable as death. Sometimes it sneaks up on you so slowly you don't notice, but it's just as likely to grab you by the hair and slap your face.

There are more medical terms now than when I was a boy. People used to suffer with their nerves – but now they're bi-polar, stressed, autistic, dyslexic, attention deficient, traumatised and compulsively obsessively disorderly. The obverse is there are any amount of syndromes around these days; the converse is there's therapy, counselling, psychiatrists and experts in mental health issues.

I didn't want counselling. I didn't care if I was apathetic. My wife seemed more interested in her keep fit class than in my melancholia – and who could blame her for leaving me? After all, girls just want to have fun – and I was no longer providing her with any; quite the reverse in fact. My friends told me to seek help, to snap out of it, to go and get drunk, to pull myself together – and then one by one they slipped off the radar and I was left with just my grey vista, my cigarettes and my whisky. In some ways it was life in a parallel universe – until the 16th of November. That was a Tuesday – and it started like any other.

I woke at 6.00 a.m. wondering how many more days I'd wake at 6.00 a.m. I pulled on a pair of jogging bottoms. I didn't shave – I wasn't too big on personal hygiene at that point. I went downstairs and made a cup of coffee then stood at the back door and lit a cigarette. It was a cold, clear, crisp morning with the moon shining her once removed reflected sunlight down on a jagged white frost. Nothing stirred until a postman appeared.

What was a postman doing at my back door at 6.15 in the morning when in the normal course of events he'd be at my front door at about 11.00?

'Arsehole?' he enquired with a cheery grin.

'What!' I spluttered.

'Are you Mister Arsehole?' Before I could answer he showed me the letter he was holding in his hand. 'This is 39 Clarion Street isn't it?'

I could see the addressee was a Mr R. Sole. 'This is number 39,' I said.

His grin widened. 'Thank you,' he said, handing me the missive and walking up the path whistling The Isle of Capri.

'But –' I began, before my voice tapered off with a whimper.

Closing the door, I tore open the envelope to find a business card inside which read, HOTLINE TO HAPPINESS

– OPEN 24 HOURS and a five digit telephone number – which made no sense at all as there should have been ten or eleven digits in my experience.

Notwithstanding the complete illogic of the situation, I gave myself up to human folly and proceeded to pick up my landline and punch in the relevant digits. It rang twice before an exuberant female voice intoned: 'Thank you for calling the Hotline to Happiness, Mr Lawrence. Someone will be with you shortly.' With that the line went dead. I was in the process of re-dialling, somewhat perplexed as to how the girl had known my name, when the front doorbell rang – and this all before 6.30 in the morning.

Putting the phone down I went to the door and upon opening it found a smartly dressed young woman with a briefcase standing in front of me.

'Good morning, Mr Lawrence,' she said, and I was immediately struck by the remarkable similarity between her voice and the girl I had just listened to on the phone.

'Good morning,' I replied, trying to make it sound as vague as I could – given the paucity of syllables involved.

'You called?'

'Did I?'

'Hotline to Happiness,' she smiled, flashing a card in front of my nose. I should have told you she was very beautiful with long, flowing auburn curls, deep blue velvet eyes and an expansive red lipsticked mouth. I confess I was taken off my guard. 'All right to come in?' she asked, with one foot already over the threshold. I opened my mouth – then closed the door behind us. There was no requirement to tell her to make herself at home – as she was already sitting in my favourite armchair.

'It's a bad business,' she said, opening up her briefcase.

'Business is bad is it?' I said – by way of saying something.

'Oh no!' she said with a wide-eyed look of infinite sadness. 'Business is positively booming.'

'Even in a recession?'

'Especially in a recession,' she replied. 'Now,' she continued, pulling out a quire of papers from her case and running her eyes over them, 'it seems your wife still loves you – so that's something you can use.'

'I beg your pardon?' I said, wondering if I had finally stepped over the line into insanity.

She looked up from her papers absent-mindedly. 'Your wife still loves you,' she repeated quite matter-of-factly before resuming her perusal, '– but there's a bit of work to be done before you try to cross that bridge. I see from my notes that you smoke.'

'Yes.'

'And you have a penchant for malt whisky.'

'Yes.'

'Well we don't see any requirement for you to give them up completely –'

'That's a bonus.'

'– but you should seriously consider taking both in moderation.'

'Are you a doctor?' I enquired.

'No,' she replied. 'You should also get rid of your television set.'

'I see.'

'It's common sense really.'

'Of course.'

'I have a few questions I'd like you to answer.'

'I thought we were already doing that.'

'The others were just pre-emptory to the main issue.'

'OK – fire away,' I said, settling back in my chair.

'What do you see there?' she asked, pointing to my settee.

'A settee,' I replied.

She ticked a box on her paper. 'And there?'

'My old Queen Anne chair.'

'And there?'

'A hearth rug.'

She made a few notes with her pen.

'OK so far?' I asked.

'Nothing unusual for a man in your condition.'

'I'm glad to hear it.'

'It's quite common – given what you've lost.'

'Lost?'

'Now – would you mind moving over to the settee please?'

'If that's what you want, who am I to refuse?' I replied complying with her request.

'No – not there – on the armrest if you don't mind.'

'You want me to sit on the armrest?'

'If you don't mind,' she simpered.

I perched myself on the armrest with my feet dangling over the edge. 'Is this OK?'

'That's ideal,' she said. 'I'm just going to join you – and I'll be putting my arms around you, purely as a precautionary measure.'

The idea was not without an inherent appeal, but I felt I had to say something. 'I think I can manage to sit here safely on my own.'

'Nonetheless,' she replied getting behind me and clasping me round the waist. 'Comfortable?' It wasn't the word I would have used – but I nodded my agreement. 'Good. What I want you to do now is to just close your eyes and relax.'

'OK,' I replied.

'Can you see anything?'

On a list of one hundred stupid questions that would come near the top.

'Nope.'

'Hmm.' She sounded vexed. 'I'm going to whisper in your ear – there's no need to be alarmed.' Alarmed I most certainly was not – though my pulse rate was increasing. 'Can you see it?' she whispered.

'See what?'

'The track.'

'Track?'

'Can you smell the smoke?'

'What?'

'Can you hear the engine? Hear the wheels? Hear the whistle blow?'

At that a screen switched on in my head and I found myself at the controls of a steam train. 'Jesus Christ!'

'Ha! Ha!' she laughed. 'You're there! You made it! Stand up now and open your eyes.'

I did – and the train was gone. 'What was that?' I said incredulously.

'No questions at the moment please. I'd like you to sit on the chair now.' I was too dumbfounded to do anything but oblige her. 'The other way,' she said.

'Facing the back?'

'Yes – and hold on to the back – tightly.' I took hold of the wooden back and she took hold of me. 'Close your eyes again. Can you see it?' In the darkness something was stirring. 'Can you smell it?' A tang of sweat assailed my nostrils. 'Can you hear them? They're chasing you!'

All at once I was hurtling through the Arizona desert on a horse with a band of Indians in hot pursuit who were whooping as if I was John Wayne. 'Bloody hell!'

'That's it – ride! Ride!' she shouted behind me. 'Now – up!' She pulled me unceremoniously from the chair and we both fell onto the floor.

'Am I going mad?' I asked.

'Oh no,' she chuckled. 'You're making great progress – and we're just in the right place for the final test,' she said patting the hearth rug. 'Just take hold of the edges – and once again I'll be taking hold of you. Now close your eyes once more – let your mind relax and tell me what you see.'

I felt the wind first, then saw clouds on the horizon – then we were off! We were sailing through those clouds on a magic carpet ride. She was laughing – a great joyful laugh full of the wonder of life and it was so infectious I found myself laughing too.

'How can this be?' I shouted into the wind as we hurtled past a flock of exotic birds.

'This is how it should be!' she yelled in my ear, hugging me close to her – before rolling us both off the carpet and back to reality.

'I think you'll be much better now,' she went on, fixing her skirt and her hair.

'How did you do that?' I asked in amazement.

'I didn't do anything,' she replied. 'You did it.'

'I don't understand.'

'Don't you remember when you were a child?'

'Some of it.'

'Remember when a settee could be a train? When a chair could be a horse? When a carpet could be magic and fly? Don't you remember when you had an imagination?'

'Yes,' I said quietly. 'I do remember.'

'That's what you lost. That's why your world turned to dust. You lost your imagination – and with it your sense of wonder.'

A warm glow suffused through my entire body as an ecstasy of understanding enveloped me.

'I'm going to be alright,' I whispered to myself. She smiled her big, beautiful smile. 'Who are you?' I asked.

'Let's just say I'm your dream girl,' she replied, placing her lips to my cheek.

The ring of the alarm clock woke me with a start.

A SNAIL'S PACE

'GOOD of you to phone me,' said John Wilson.

'Good of you to invite me over,' Tom Dempsey replied as he sat down.

'I got some real ale on offer at the supermarket. You up for one?'

'Sounds good to me – got to be better than the chemical mix they sell in the pub.'

'So what's been happening since …' John's voiced trailed off as he struggled to remember the last time they'd met.

'Yes – must be almost a year since Alan's wedding. I know we occasionally e-mail and text but we really should get together face to face more often,' said Tom opening his beer. 'Cheers.'

'Cheers.'

They sat a moment, savouring that first mouthful.

'As to what's been happening – not a lot. Still struggling to pay the bills as a self-employed joiner. How about you?'

'Took early retirement a few months back.'

'You lucky bastard!'

'Well – not much coming in, but enough to keep the wolf from the door – and no more work hassles.'

'You filling in your time OK?'

'I never had any problem with that.'

'You always did have lots of interests – in fact that's the reason I wanted to see you,' said Tom.

'My interests?'

'Are you still into all that Fortean Times and Arthur C. Clarke's World Of Strange Powers stuff?'

'Up to a point. I stick the odd outré newspaper clipping in a scrapbook now and then – why?'

'I had a rather outré experience of my own that I'd like to run by you – I think it's the sort of thing that might light your candle.'

'Fire away,' said John eagerly.

'Do you remember Jimmy Arbuckle from school?'

'Arbuckle?' said John with a frown. 'Arbuckle?'

'Tall thin guy,' said Tom, trying to nudge his memory. 'Specs, long hair …'

'Ah! Always had a Deep Purple album under his arm?' said John as the penny dropped.

'That's him.'

'Not the sharpest knife in the drawer as I recall,' John mused.

'No, I think he was a couple of classes below us. Anyway – I was in the pub a couple of months back and who should be sitting across from me but –'

'Jimmy Arbuckle.'

'Exactly – only now he's fat, baldy and the only deep purple thing about him are the veins in his nose.'

'Likes a drink then?'

'Or four. Well – we looked across the room, both

recognising that we knew each other from somewhere and although we were never great cronies at school we reintroduced ourselves and were soon travelling full speed down memory lane recalling old teachers and pupils.'

'Interesting – but not really outré,' said John.

'There's more,' said Tom. 'After a few rounds we were both wallowing in nostalgia and remembering Christine Kellerman and what we'd have liked to have done with her.'

'She was hot!'

'Finally we exhausted that avenue and I got up to get another round in. When I came back he had his mobile phone sitting on the table.'

'Nothing too strange in that,' said Tom.

'No – granted,' John replied. 'But then he lowers his voice and starts telling me a bizarre tale in what can only be described as a conspiratorial tone.'

'Concerning?'

'The gist of the story was that he's in the habit of getting up early in the morning and smoking a cigarette sitting on the back step of his house.'

'I'm with you so far.'

'Well, one day he's sitting there as usual when he looks down at the slabs and sees the trail of a snail.'

'Rambling in the night no doubt.'

'No doubt – but the thing about this trail is that it's in the shape of a man's head and shoulders – and he's wearing a bowler hat …'

'What!'

'… And he's got a knife through his neck.'

'How many whiskeys did he have the night before?' laughed John.

'My thoughts exactly – but then he picks up his phone and shows me the picture he took of it.'

'You saw it?'

'Yes – it was the outline of the head and shoulders of a man in a bowler hat with a knife through his neck.'

'That's certainly a bit off the beaten track.'

'You haven't heard the half of it.'

John stopped in mid sip. 'Didn't that gang boss in Boston …'

'Lucky Eddie?'

'That's him! Didn't he wear a bowler hat? I remember seeing his photo in the paper.'

'Two days after Jimmy took the snap of his slabs, Lucky Eddie Capriati's luck ran out when he was stabbed though the neck during an all-night poker game.'

'That's quite a coincidence – his trademark being the bowler hat and all,' said John.

'Coincidence indeed,' Tom remarked. 'A couple of weeks later Jimmy's out early again and this time there's a trail in the shape of a plane – heading downwards.'

'The one in the Azores?'

'Two days later that 747 plunges into the sea off the Azores with no survivors.'

'Jesus! Any more?'

'Just what I was going to ask you,' said Tom shaking his empty bottle. More refreshment being provided he continued with his narrative. 'Of course I saw his pic of the plane snail trail too and then he says that on that very morning we met he had found another one.'

'What was it this time?' asked John.

'He flicks his phone and there's the outline of a horse with the number six in the middle of it.'

'I don't know much about horses – or horseracing.'

'I've lost enough in my time to realise I don't know much either but Jimmy tells me the Derby will be running two days later and he'll be putting every penny he can raise on whatever is number six in the race.'

'And did he?'

'I'll get to that in the course of events.'

'Sorry.'

'By this time we're both pretty pissed and it's time to shake hands and say goodnight with the obligatory we must meet up again soon stuff. On the day of the race I look at the paper and check out the form of number six – which is called Brian's Tale.'

'Brian – the snail from The Magic Roundabout!'

'I think that's just a bridge too far there. Anyway – this Brian's Tale looks as if it couldn't win a seller at Sedgefield never mind the Derby – and it's standing at 100/1.'

'Did you bet it yourself?'

'Nope – no one in their right mind would have bet it. The tape goes up 'They're off!' and Brian's Tale is all but left in the stalls. Finally it decides to show its face – about ten lengths behind everything else – and as the race progresses it gets further and further behind.'

'I sense a but …'

'But suddenly, as they're rounding Tattenham Corner, the favourite slips, falls on its arse and creates carnage behind it bringing down three and causing another two to unseat their riders.'

'Like the Foinavon Grand National?'

'Exactly like that – then up plods Brian's Tale in true Foinavon fashion and trots past then all up to the winning line.'

'Bloody hell! At 100/1?'

'Nope – it was 150/1 on the day. I didn't know whether to be sick in the sink or concentrate on my diarrhoea in the loo.'

'So do you think Jimmy got his bet on?'

'Here's something for your scrapbook,' Tom replied going into his wallet and handing John a piece of paper.

'Obituary! So he's dead?'

'I saw that in the paper last week.'

'Says, 'Suddenly' …'

'It was. Of course I went to the funeral yesterday and got talking to a few faces. Seems he was on honeymoon down South with some Essex girl he had married and fell out of a sixteenth-storey hotel window while he was celebrating his nuptials.'

'Did you see the girl?'

'Yes – short black skirt, permatan, loads of cleavage, shades on.'

'Not the grieving widow type then?'

'She said all the right things and blew her nose and dabbed beneath her sunglasses a few times but by the end of the tea she seemed to have taken quite a fancy to Jimmy's young cousin.'

'That's certainly a strange tale,' said John.

'Not quite done yet.'

'No?'

'I was walking through the town yesterday and decided to take a look at Jimmy's old house. I don't think he had ever moved – his parents had bought it when he was in his twenties. It was easy enough to find – the only one with a 'For Sale' sign stuck in the front lawn. Seeing that made me feel a bit bolder so I opened the gate and tried to look like a potential buyer as I toddled round to his back door.'

'Anything interesting there?'

'Just this,' said Tom pulling out his phone and displaying the grainy image of a tall building with one matchstick figure halfway down the outside of it and another figure inside near the top with its arms extended and what could be construed as a grin on its face …

JOHN

BY the age of eight Kevin had been diagnosed as being both autistic and dyslexic, on top of which it had been concluded that he suffered from dual disorders, namely Attention Deficiency and Gender Identity. But one Sunday morning in June all that changed.

'Can I have Coco Pops, Mum?' Kevin asked.

'I'd rather you didn't Kevin. You know they're full of sugar – and sugar's bad for you,' said Mary Bridges, mentally taking a step backwards to prepare herself for the onset of the inevitable tantrum.

'OK,' said Kevin, 'I'll have Corn Flakes instead.'

To say that Mr and Mrs Bridges were taken aback would be to seriously understate matters.

'Are you feeling all right, Kevin?' his mother asked.

'Yes – I'm fine now.'

'Now?'

'Yes – John told me stuff and I feel a lot better now.'

'John?' said his father. 'John who?'

'John Dawes – he's my friend,' said Kevin pouring milk on his cereal.

'Did you meet him at school?' asked his mother.

'No – he doesn't go to school. Can I have some toast, Mum?'

'Of course,' Mrs Bridges beamed.

'Thanks.'

Did she hear right? Did her son just say 'Thanks' for the first time in his life? She looked across the table at her husband to find his jaw had dropped.

'Are you quite sure you're feeling all right, Kevin?'

'Mm hmm,' her son mumbled through his cereal.

'Does John live locally?' asked his father.

'I suppose so,' Kevin replied.

'You suppose so?'

'He's always around.'

'Why doesn't he go to school?' asked Mrs Bridges.

'Dunno.'

'Do his parents know he doesn't go to school?' she went on anxiously.

'Dunno.'

'You don't seem to know very much about John at all.'

'I only met him last week – he's helping me with my times tables.'

'What!' Mr Bridges exclaimed.

'You know – twelve ones are twelve, twelve twos are twenty-four, twelve threes are thirty-six, twelve fours are …'

'You could never do that before, Kevin!' said his astounded mother.

Kevin gave a shrug. 'John made it make sense – and he says dressing up as a girl is cissy – so I don't want to do that any more.'

To his parents it appeared that John had achieved more in a week than a battalion of child psychologists had managed in four years.

'Please may I leave the table now, Mum?' her son asked.

'What do you mean?' his father asked suspiciously, wondering if the fairies had substituted an elfin child for theirs in the night.

'John says it's good to show manners.'

'Your new friend sounds like a very sensible boy. Your dad and I would love to meet him – why don't you bring him round to tea?'

Kevin gave a grimace. 'John's kind of shy – he doesn't like meeting people,' he replied.

'But he must like you,' said his mother.

'I think we like each other,' Kevin agreed.

'What age is John?' Mr Bridges enquired.

'Sixteen.'

'Sixteen!' cried his horrified mother, with images of child abuse in her head. 'He's far too old to be your friend, Kevin. And what did I tell you about never talking to strangers.'

'But didn't you say a stranger is just a friend you don't know yet?' said the bemused Kevin.

'Yes – well,' his mother stammered with a cough, 'But that's… different.'

'How's it different?'

'Never you mind – it just is!' she snapped.

'John says mums and dads don't always make sense. I think he's right,' said her son.

'Are you seeing John today?' asked his father.

'I 'spect so. He's going to show me how to do fishing.'

'Fishing?' said Mr Bridges, aware there was no water nearby. 'Where?'

'Not to any rivers or such – he's just going to tell me about it – explain it like. John's good at explaining things. I understand him better than my teachers.'

'I don't think you should get to like John too much,' said his mum.

'Why? John's my friend.'

'Where are you meeting him?' his father asked.

'Dunno – he always finds me. Can I go now please, Mum?'

'Did you take your medication?'

'No,' her son replied. 'John says I don't need no pills any more. I didn't take any yesterday neither.'

'That's very naughty of you, Kevin – you know you need to take your tablets to keep you ... feeling well,' said Mrs Bridges.

'But I feel much better now not taking them,' argued Kevin – and in truth, given what his parents had just witnessed they didn't have the heart to argue back.

'Should we phone the doctor, Tom?' asked the worried Mrs Bridges as Kevin ambled out into the backyard.

'I don't know whether to phone the doctor or go to chapel and light a candle,' said her husband. 'He's a new lad – it's incredible.'

'It doesn't seem right though,' his wife replied anxiously.

'It seems all bloody right to me,' said Tom Bridges. 'Let's run with it and see where it goes.'

II

Mary was doing the washing up a couple of hours later when she looked through the window to find her son walking along talking animatedly – to no one.

'Oh my God!' she gasped.

Kevin was laughing – and pushing against something – suddenly he fell on the grass, still laughing.

'Yeah – I'll see you tomorrow,' he cried with a grin. 'I'll get you back!'

His mother said nothing of it when he walked in.

'Did you have a good time?' she asked.

'Yes – it was fun,' Kevin replied.

'Did you … see John today?'

'Yes, he taught me loads about fishing,' her son replied enthusiastically. 'He knows loads of stuff. Do we have a Bible, Mum?'

'A Bible? What do you want with a Bible?' said the astonished Mrs Bridges.

'John says it's a good thing to read – it's good practise for reading cos it's got lots of good stories and stuff. He says there's a book by someone called Homer too – not Homer Simpson – he says that's good to read too. Do you know that book? John told me – but I forget.'

'The Odyssey?'

'That's it! cried Kevin. 'John says it's really exciting. Do you think it'll be in the library?'

'I'd imagine they'll be able to get a copy for you,' said his mother quietly. 'Go and wash up now – tea's almost ready.'

'OK Mum.' He moved to her and hugged her. Tears came to her eyes.

'What's that for?' she gulped.

He smiled bashfully, turned his head away shyly and said, 'Oh – you know,' before bounding up the stairs with a gleeful laugh.

III

'There's really nothing to worry about,' said Dr Feldstein to Kevin's concerned parents a few days later. 'Imaginary friends are part and parcel of many children's development. They offer scope for role-playing and allow the child to attain a better understanding of the adult world. They also provide additional linguistic practise as the child is talking and interacting with his or her pretend companion.'

'So you don't think there's anything wrong with Kevin?' said Mary.

'It's a very common occurrence, Mrs Bridges,' smiled the doctor. 'I'm sure that – John, is it? Yes, I'm sure that in the course of time John will disappear just as quickly as he arrived.'

The doctor's prognosis proved to be correct sooner than Kevin's parents could have hoped for, as a week later their downcast son walked in and announced that John was moving away that day.

'Oh,' said Mrs Bridges, 'what a shame – I'd so like to have met him. Is he moving far?'

'He don't know.'

'He doesn't know where he's moving to?'

'No – he just knows he has to go.'

It sounded a bit puzzling to Mary but she simply replied, 'You'll miss him, won't you?'

'Yes,' said the boy with his lip trembling.

His mother hugged him close to her. 'Never mind – it was good that you became friends.'

'Yes,' said Kevin. 'He was the best friend I ever had.' His face suddenly brightened, 'And he says we'll meet up again someday.'

IV

Seven months later Tom and Mary Bridges had just left church.

'It was a good service,' said Mary.

'I'll need to get back to work soon – it's not as if she was family.'

'Tom! We've lived two doors down from her for six years. The least we can do is go to the cemetery. She was a lovely old biddy – she thought the world of Kevin.'

Her husband sighed. 'OK – but I'm not going to the tea.'

'No – we'll just go to the cemetery,' his wife agreed.

By the time they reached it a fine, drizzly rain had begun to fall.

'Bloody typical,' said Tom, 'And we didn't bring a brolly.'

'We'll not be here long,' said Mary. 'Come on.'

She took his hand and they walked slowly up the

winding path to where the burial was to take place. Mary's eyes perused the gravestones as they passed them. It was a sombre sight – to see all those hopes, dreams, aspirations and ambitions all come to the same end – though somehow rather comforting in a strange way. Suddenly she stopped in her tracks and gave a gasp.

'What?' Tom asked. 'What's wrong?'

She said nothing, but simply pointed to a nearby headstone. Her short-sighted husband took a step forward and read the inscription upon it.

John Dawes
1870 – 1886
RIP

I here will slumber underground
Until the last loud trump will sound
Then burst my tomb with sweet surprise
And in my saviour's image rise.

THE LOST CHORD

I

WHEN I was a schoolboy music lessons were simply a once a week opportunity to sing along lustily to Men of Harlech while our teacher, a baldy old rapscallion by the name of Mr Traynor, belted it out on the piano accompanied by the odd slam from his walking stick when he felt we weren't giving it our all.

It was the one period in the week where various classes came together and the only time I was in contact with Martin Boyd. Despite that fact we saw something in each other and formed a close bond for a spell. Martin was a quiet, shy boy. He'd doubtless be classified as autistic these days. He rarely spoke unless a direct question was asked of him.

I recall one time, old Traynor being called away for whatever reason, when the subject of our juvenile conversation turned to, 'What Do You Think The Weirdest Thing In The World Is?' as we filled in the time till his return. One said the Abominable Snowman, another said Siamese twins, another opted for feral children reared by wolves in the wild. When it came Martin's turn to answer he replied deadpan, 'The change from a major to a minor chord.' As thirteen-year-olds we were singularly unimpressed by this – indeed I don't suppose more than a handful knew what he was talking about – and I include myself in the role of ignoramus. I asked him about it afterwards.

'What's the change from a major to a minor chord?'

'It's when the feel changes from happy to sad. Haven't you ever noticed?' he replied. I must have looked blank. 'Come round tonight and I'll show you.'

As it turned out I was unable to go to his place that evening, as my father had won a tenner on the horses and was taking us out for a fish supper. Those were the days!

In the meantime, by one of those strange quirks of synchronicity, my sister was playing an Ella Fitzgerald LP in her bedroom while she was dolling herself up to go to the Saturday night dancing. It was quite a shock to hear her singing along to:

'There's no love song finer,
But how strange the change from major to minor.
Every time we say goodbye.'

'What does that mean?' I asked.

'I dunno,' she replied. 'It's just a song – hand me over that compact will you?'

So it came to pass that I was none the wiser by the time I caught up with Martin at his house the following week.

'You were gonna tell me about that major and minor thing,' I reminded him.

'Oh yes,' he said. 'Come on.'

I followed him into the sitting room where the piano sat.

'Listen,' he said, then struck three notes together. 'Major. Now, listen again.' He struck another three notes. 'Minor. Hear the difference?' He played both several times saying, 'Happy – sad – happy – sad – happy – sad.' He was right. I nodded my head.

'That is a bit – weird.'

'It's the weirdest thing in the world,' he replied.

'I dunno if it's that weird!' I said.

'Music is the soul of the world embedded in sound,' he said quietly, then began to play.

He'd had no formal tuition at all – he just had a great ear. I know now it was Beethoven's Moonlight Sonata he played at first – I didn't know anything about that at the time – but the music painted a melancholy picture of moonlight on water in my head. After that he played a piece by Satie. Again I had no conception of either the composer or the piece, but in my mind an oppressive sense of both longing and foreboding took hold and I glimpsed a vision of a distant Arcadian green land where the Great God Pan yet ruled.

As if aware of the dark depths to which he had taken me, Martin finished off with a hell for leather version of the Beatles Get Back and normal service was resumed. But those few brief minutes had showed me the power of music – an intense power that struck deep at our natural emotions.

He lowered the lid onto the keys then turned to me.

'I want to find something here no one else has,' he said solemnly with his hand on the piano.

'What? Like the lost chord?' I replied, recalling the title of my sister's Moody Blues LP.

His eyes lit up and a huge smile spread across his face.

'Yes!' he beamed. 'That's it! – I need to find the lost chord!'

II

It wasn't long after that when Martin's parents divorced and his mother took him with her to live in Edinburgh. I genuinely missed him, as he had opened up a new world to me when he played that afternoon. I became much more serious about listening to music and even bought a guitar and began to create my own. I was never a superstar, but I've made a living out of it for over thirty years, playing in pubs, clubs and various festivals. I owe it all to Martin – in a way I even owe my wife and kids to him because without music I would never have met Maureen.

I often thought about my old school friend and the effect he had on my life. I wondered what his life had been like. It was hard to imagine Martin with an office job and a wife and children. It was when I was in Edinburgh doing a festival gig that I finally got some answers.

The gig was an afternoon one and after the show I wandered into one of the pubs on the Royal Mile to relax with a pint or two. It was packed of course – they all are during the Festival. As I made my way in, someone was being thrown out.

'You've had enough, pal – time to go home.'

The drunk wasn't in a fighting mood. He went quietly and slumped down on a bench outside. Normally I wouldn't have given it a thought and just left him there to get on with it, but there was something in his posture – something that switched a light on in the attic of my memory.

'Are you all right, mate?' I asked, patting him on the shoulder. He lifted his head slowly and tried to focus on me.

'Eh?'

A rush of adrenalin pumped through me. It was Martin! He looked a hundred years old – but it was Martin!

'Martin!' I cried. 'Martin Boyd!' He spun back, aghast that someone should be addressing him by name. 'It's Jamie – Jamie Douglas.'

His eyes narrowed and then opened wide in shock.

'Jamie,' he slurred – then gasped again, 'Jamie!'

With that he threw his arms around me and wept like a child.

It took me ten minutes to understand what he was saying when I asked for his address and another ten to flag down a taxi. The driver was unwilling to take us at first, but when he saw I at least was sober he agreed, on the understanding that I would pay for any mess that Martin might make on the journey, to which I was happy to concur.

We were no sooner out of the cab than Marin threw up violently into a nearby wheelie bin – which fortunately turned out to be his own. I helped him up the stairs to his flat and found the door key in his pocket.

The place was a shambles. I had to clear takeaway trays

from the broken settee to sit him down. His head slumped and I saw he was asleep. I opened all the windows in an attempt to rout the foetid atmosphere and then spent the next half hour carting rubbish from his flat to the bin downstairs. The smell of the coffee I was making roused him from his slumber. Evacuating his stomach again down the toilet bowl was his first task.

'Jesus,' he mumbled, stumbling back to his chair. I gave him a coffee and he slurped at it greedily. 'Bloody Hell!' he announced, to no one in particular, before opening his eyes. 'Jamie – aw Jamie.' His hand reached out and grabbed mine. His head shook from side to side – he was breathing heavily. A wan smile came to his lips. 'Jamie,' he said. 'Imagine. You got any fags?'

I'd given up smoking years ago, but I'd found a half full packet during my clean-up of the flat which I now handed over.

'I just want one,' he said.

'They're yours – I found them under a week old curry.'

'Cheers,' he replied lighting up. He was actually sobering up fast. Vomiting has its compensations.

'So,' I said, 'what's been happening with you?' – at which we both laughed.

'It's great to see you, Jamie,' he said. 'You don't know how great.'

'How did things – ?' I gestured around the room.

'It wasn't always like this.' He drew himself up with mock pride. 'I'll have you know I was a postman.'

'A postman?'

'Aye – and a bloody good one too for twenty years.'

'I can believe it – tenacity was always one of your strong points. You'd have made sure the Pony Express got through.'

His mood grew more sombre.

'You'll be thinking it's the drink – or worse,' he said, 'and it's true I go on benders, but it's the only way I can escape.'

'We've all used drink as a form of escape.'

He laughed gently. 'Aye – we've all got different jailers.'

'Who's yours?' I asked.

'He's behind you,' he replied.

I turned around. 'The piano?'

'The bane of my bloody life!' he spat with a vengeance.

'Why?' I asked, puzzled.

A few seconds passed before he replied, as if he was gathering his thoughts and putting them in order.

'Do you remember when we were kids we once talked about majors and minors – and the lost chord?'

'I'll never forget that afternoon,' said I. 'It changed my life. I've made my living from music for thirty years.'

'Really?' he said, surprised – and a spark of the boy I once knew was in his eyes. 'What do you play?'

'Guitar.'

'Do your own stuff?'

'Yes.'

'That's great!'

'And it's all down to you. It was that afternoon in your house that gave me the push.'

'That's interesting,' Martin said quietly. 'Yes – that's very interesting – because it was you mentioning the lost chord that set me on a journey to find it.'

'Sorry to waste your time,' I laughed, moving towards the piano and playing a C major chord – only it wasn't a C major chord that rang out. 'I think you need it tuned,' I said.

'I've tuned it myself – to my own specifications.'

'What?'

'I daresay you know that the guitar can be tuned in different ways.'

'Yes, of course – I use some of them occasionally,' I said. 'But a piano?'

'Sit down,' he said softly. 'I'll play for you.'

We exchanged places and he rested his fingers on the keyboard. 'Don't fall asleep,' he said.

'Will it be that boring?' I joked.

'Stay alert, Jamie – this could be a bad idea.'

'What are you talking about?' I replied with a nervous laugh.

I noticed that his pale, nervous fingers were trembling prior to moving on the keys, but they grew in confidence – and arrogance – as a melody began to form. It was strange from the outset – quite literally unworldly – like music you would find in another world, on another planet. As it continued on I felt myself slowly withdrawing from my own inner psyche. The notes seemed to float in the air, like soap bubbles blown by a precocious child – yet they were no notes at all – they were what lies in the limbo between the notes – they were the intervals between the intervals.

I began to feel drowsy. Something was happening in my

head – cloudy visions, half-formed flashbacks. I had tried LSD only once in my life and it reminded me of that – only much more powerful. I saw Eden – Paradise – I understood! Yet for all the beauty that assailed my senses, my instincts were pulling me in another direction – where something of the night lurked hidden behind the backdrop. I felt that one wrong note could bring forth terrors that no man could face. Here were worlds within worlds; the magisterial yin and yang; the ebb and flow of eternities – and, lurking in between those notes – unspeakable horrors!

My eyelids began to droop and a flash of something hit my optic nerve. It was beyond ancient, beyond time – and beyond evil. In vain I tried to fight against the whoreson lethargy that permeated my very soul – it was impossible to resist. Again my eyes closed and such a dread fell upon me that I thought I should be grateful to die then and there. I was led in, drawn in, sucked in. My aghast senses could not conceive of such abominations as they were being forced to face. It was a vision of appalling, dire horror beyond human comprehension! How I finally broke the mesmeric spell that held me there I do not know. It was not willpower that did it – for I had none. To this day I believe some … thing intervened on my behalf.

I was brought back from the brink of absolute petrification and despair, as if by a bolt of lightning striking me, to find Martin with his eyes closed, sweat running down his brow, his fingers still floating up and down the keyboard. Jumping up like a man possessed, I made a grab for the heaviest thing I could find – which happened to be a fire extinguisher of all things. Squeezing the nozzle as hard as I could I watched with glee as it burst into life, flooding the inner workings of the piano with foam in an instant. But that wasn't enough for me. Thrusting my friend aside I proceeded to use the extinguisher as a hammer to batter the instrument again and again until it lay in pieces all around us. At last exhaustion kicked in and I collapsed into a chair where Martin and I faced each other like two boxers who have gone fifteen rounds together.

'I told you not to fall asleep,' he said, with what I think was his idea of a smile.

'What the hell have you done?'

His voice sunk to a whisper, 'Found the lost chord.'

We sat in silence for a minute. I took the cigarette he offered me.

'Do you remember how it was tuned?' I asked as he lit it.

He shook his head. 'I've got it written down though.'

'Find it,' I said.

He rose and went into another room, returning with a small notebook. 'It's in there,' he said.

'Show me.'

He turned a few pages. 'There.'

'Is it written down anywhere else?' I asked.

'No,' he replied.

Ripping the pages from the book I picked up his lighter and set fire to them then watched as they burned up in the ashtray.

'I could have been famous,' he said with mock chagrin.

I was in no mood for humour.

'Will you … will we be free of it?' I asked.

He nodded. 'It's a hell of a memory though.'

'You're a genius,' I said.

'I'd rather be a postman,' he replied.

'I'm sure you can be that again,' I said, stubbing out my cigarette and slapping him on the back. 'Come on – let's go somewhere for an expensive Edinburgh Festival coffee.'

THE VOICE OF EXPERIENCE

ANDREW was getting frustrated. It was all very well to have a shiny new guitar – but the fact was he had no idea how to play it. It was true he had learned a few chords from the book he had bought but he really wanted someone to show him more.

'There's John Davies – he teaches,' said his friend Jim.

'But he teaches notes and reading – I don't want all that.'

'What about the guy who has his number in the paper?'

'That's reading music too.'

'The only other person I ever saw round here with a guitar is that old guy who moved into number 47 just down the road from me.'

'Who's that?'

'I dunno his name,' said Jim. 'He's only been there a couple of weeks – looks like an old jakey – but I saw him through the window when I was passing once and he was holding a guitar.'

'Same street as you?'

'Yes – just around the corner – number 47.'

'I'll check it out.'

'Better tell your mum you're going – this guy looks a bit… out there.'

Andrew didn't tell his mother. He simply walked round next day and knocked on the door of number 47. It was eventually opened by a fat, baldy, dishevelled looking, cigarette smoking middle-aged man in a vest and jogging bottoms.

'Yeah?' he coughed.

'Do you play the guitar?'

There was a pause. 'Yeah.'

'Do you give lessons?'

'Lessons?'

'I'd like someone to show me. I'll pay – as long as they don't cost too much,' he added, thinking of his strained financial resources.

The man took a long draw on his cigarette. 'You got a guitar?' he said at last.

'Yes.'

'Bring it round tomorrow afternoon.' With that he closed the door.

The place was a mess – even a teenager like Andrew could see that.

'What's your name?' the man asked.

'Andrew.'

'Andrew, eh?'

'What's yours?'

'Sonny.'

'Sonny?'

'Yeah – what's wrong with that?'

'Nothing – it just sounds more like a nickname than a real one.'

'Well I've been called Sonny since I joined the Navy – when I was just a little older than you I reckon. Are you eighteen?'

'Seventeen,' said Andrew.

'What kind of music do you like?'

'I like the old blues.'

'Yeah? Well that's good cause I like them too. OK – get your guitar and let's see what we can do.'

'How much will it cost?' Andrew asked.

'It won't cost nothing, son.'

'I don't want it for nothing.'

'Well it's either that or you won't be getting taught nothing.'

Andrew paused to consider his options, then said, 'Thanks.'

'What's he like?' asked Jim.

'He's OK – kind of grumpy at times – but he's a great guitar player – knows tons of stuff.'

'What's his house like?'

'Yucky,' said Andrew. 'Smells of fags and whisky – he always has a drink on the table.'

'I'm never going to smoke,' said Jim.

'Me neither,' said Andrew. 'Or drink.'

'Me neither,' said Jim.

'That's it for today,' said Sonny. 'Go home and learn that and we'll see if you can play it on Wednesday.'

'I won't be able to make it on Wednesday.'

'No? Why's that?'

'I've applied to go to university and there's an Open Day.'

'So have you been accepted for uni?'

'Yes.'

'And are you going?'

'I think so.'

'Wish I'd went,' said Sonny with a sigh as he lit another cigarette.

'Did you have the chance?'

'Yeah – I was accepted.'

'What happened?' asked Andrew.

'I met Mandy.'

'Was she your girlfriend?'

'She was – and then my wife two months after I met her. I had to get a job then – so university went out the window. You make sure you don't make the same mistake as me.'

Mandy was obviously no longer in the picture but Andrew didn't want to delve too deeply into his tutor's private life. As it was Sonny filled in the blanks for him.

'Ten years we were together – till she ran off with the Provi man while I was in Singapore.'

'Did you have a family?'

'One boy – Darren.'

'Where's he now?'

'Died in a car crash when he was twenty-two.'

'I'm sorry.' Andrew mumbled.

'It's OK – it was all a long time ago – and time's a strange thing.'

'It must have been awful having those things happen to you.'

'Yes – it was,' said Sonny sadly. 'But that's life – as you'll no doubt discover for yourself as time goes by.'

His introspection was interrupted by a knock at the door.

'Oh – that'll be my friend Jim,' said Andrew. 'He got a new camera and I asked him if he'd take a picture of us together with our guitars to send to my pen pal in New Zealand. Is that OK?'

'It's OK with me – wheel him in.'

Andrew chapped the door a second time but still got no response. It was unusual for Sonny to be out – and he had wanted to tell him about the Open Day.

'Did you go to that Open Day?' asked Jim as they sipped lemonade in the cafe later.

'Yes – it was really interesting.'

'So you're set on being a student?'

'Yep – four year course. What about you?'

'Dunno – my uncle Pat might be getting me into the steelworks – good money in there.'

The cafe door opened and two teenage girls walked in – giggling as they sat down near the two boys.

'This could be our lucky day,' whispered Jim with a nudge.

'I think I just fell in love,' said Andrew, staring open-mouthed across the table.

'Hi girls, I'm Jim – and this is Andrew.'

The girls giggled all the more.

'I'm Jill – and this is my friend, Mandy.'

TIME WILL TELL

CHAPTER I

MY brother and I had been living under the same roof for forty-two years when he died. Like the vast majority of deaths it came completely out of the blue. I was in the process of dipping a digestive biscuit in my mid-morning cuppa when the policeman knocked on the door and informed me of his demise.

The actual content of the conversation rather washed over me. There were disconnected phrases such as '… massive heart attack … no pain … so sorry …' which were obviously being used as part of a complete sentence – but my brain simply fed me the salient words and let the rest float by. I invited PC 1286 in and we both dunked our respective digestives as he gave me his condolences and filled me in on the details. He had died at his desk in the insurance office – simply keeled over with no warning, thereby creating his twenty-something supervisor's first 'challenge' of the day. Unfortunately she failed to 'take it on board' and was led away to an upstairs room screaming hysterically.

I heard about this later at the crematorium from one of his colleagues. But I should introduce myself before you become too embroiled within my narrative. My name is Bryson – John Bryson. It was Oscar Wilde's considered opinion that anyone who had lost both parents was guilty of being careless. I can only speculate as to what he would have made of my predicament, having lost not only a mother and father but also a sister and brother.

My sister had married some twenty-five years ago and moved to Wales and I have no doubt that my mother expected a somewhat similar fate to befall both her sons. Alas her eternal hopes were destined never to reach fruition. Having nursed my sick father – a man broken by decades of heavy work in the steelworks and hydro-electric schemes – having nursed him for seven years, until his blessed relief came, she had little enough time to enjoy her new found leisure and 'was taken' as they say but two years later. This left Peter and I to fend for ourselves three years ago for the first time in our lives. I was thirty-nine and he was forty-six.

You'll think it strange that we should still be living in the same house we were born in after all those years, but there are stranger things in the world and it would not take the gold medal. We had simply grown accustomed to a routine where we were pampered and treated like royalty. Why should we risk all our home comforts for the dubious joys of the wedding bed? I had watched the vast majority of my friends joined in holy matrimony and observed the many subtle (and not so subtle) changes that such a giant step engenders. I was in no hurry to step over the precipice. I couldn't say what Peter's opinion of it was – we were never that close. Having written that, I feel rather ashamed. I'd love to write of us going white water rafting in Canada or scuba diving off the coast of Mexico – but it never happened. Forty-two years together and at no time did we feel that lasting bond that supposedly binds brother to brother. It seems inhuman in some way – oh we talked sometimes – but only on a very superficial level, we never debated any serious issues. It's hard to say why not – that was just the way it was.

I'd been working in the bank for five years when Mum died. I knew one of us would have to take over her 'role' and I was ready to do so. I was sick of the bank; sick of the greed and the pettiness – the sales targets and the lies. I never was one of those people who need to work. I detested it. It kept me from my books, from my writing (I'd had some success in seeing my poetry published in various magazines), and from my music. I loved playing the guitar.

Peter on the other hand had no such interests. His normal weekend involved nothing more than running between the pub and the bookmakers, coming home to watch a high body count video and then going to bed. For all that he slated his insurance firm, he needed the work to give his life a purpose. With neither wife nor children he could simply work all week and then drink, smoke and gamble his earnings at the weekend. The only person he was doing any harm to was himself. That was his life.

Or so I thought. But who over forty would say that life is a straightforward business? The black and white ethics of youth grow more and more blurred with each passing year until only a dull grey vista remains – where all things are at once both possible and impossible; right and wrong; good and bad.

Afterwards, as I was washing up, PC 1286 having departed, I felt a strong urge to burst out laughing. It had all started out as a perfectly normal Tuesday morning. There was nothing different about it. Peter had got on his usual train and gone to work at his usual hour – and now he was dead. I felt a slight pique of annoyance as I thought of the six pork chops I had bought for that day's dinner. Having stopped smoking eighteen months ago I now pulled one from the almost empty pack that Peter had left on the coffee table and lit it on the electric hob of the cooker before sitting down in the living room. What did it all mean? Why was I the only one left? Why wasn't I crying? No one escapes these questions – or questions very like them. Rich and poor alike must at length drink from the same pool of despair.

CHAPTER II

The funeral took place on the Friday. The turnout took me by surprise – all the regulars from The Gates put in an appearance, as did the majority of his workmates. I was glad I'd given instructions to cater for forty.

I mixed as best I could with the motley assembly as they ate their sausage rolls and sandwiches, but I only knew a handful of people: Aunt Phyllis; Uncle Danny; a far removed cousin who I hadn't seen in fifteen years. My late sister's husband had given me his condolences over the phone and it was no surprise to me when he said he wouldn't be coming up for the funeral – if I'd been in his position I'd have done the same.

I watched as a seedy looking man with grizzled, grey hair – fifty-five, maybe older – made his way from the bar towards me. His ill-fitting suit had a general demeanour of age and decrepitude which intimated that its sole purpose in life was to bid farewell to the dead. His lips formed their idea of a smile as he introduced himself.

'Tommy Jeffries.'

'Pleased to meet you, Mr Jeffries.'

'He was a character was Peter.' He laughed as he said this – a quick, high pitched intake of breath it was, with a spasmodic shake of the head. I knew what that word meant, as do women up and down the country who are married to 'characters'. 'He'll be sorely missed,' he ended with a sigh.

I had no idea whether Mr Jeffries was acquainted with my brother through work, drink or gambling so I gave a somewhat noncommittal response which I hoped would spur him on to further clarification.

'You would only know him as a brother,' he continued – I said nothing as he took a swig from his whisky glass – 'but he was more than a brother to me – he was a fellow traveller.'

Trenchant though this comment was, it did not offer me any assistance in my search for Mr Jeffries' role in the scheme of things.

'You knew Peter well then?' I ventured.

He threw his head back with a mixture of dignity and

disdain and his weak, watery, pale blue eyes met my own. His mouth opened and I could see that he had something of a profound nature to say. It closed just as quickly and his brows narrowed quizzically. 'I'm – I'm sorry – you are?'

'John – John Bryson,' I replied.

He hailed me as an old friend. 'John! Of course – John Bryson – he spoke of you often – oh yes – and always in a deferential manner. He thought the world of you – your poetry, your music – he was very proud of you.'

It would not be untrue to say that I was more taken aback by this piece of information than I was by my brother's death. At no time had he ever shown the slightest interest in either my literary or musical compositions. He himself was completely tone deaf and preferred to read the latest American detective fiction rather than the classic novels and poetry I held so dear. Even as all this was running through my head my companion was talking.

'… Often quoted The Man in Black – you know it of course – what's his name?'

'Oliver Goldsmith.'

'That's the one – yes Peter often quoted that to us 'Though fond of many acquaintances I desire an intimacy with only with a few'. A very charming view of being anti-social, eh?'

I had no idea that my late brother was familiar with Goldsmith – but I wasn't about to admit that to Tommy Jeffries. I decided it was time to take the bull by the horns.

'I'm sorry – I'm not quite sure how you came to be acquainted with my brother.'

'Oh, I've known him for many years. He and I–'

'A good turnout,' said my aunt Phyllis, bursting through the throng by the door. 'I see Robert couldn't be bothered coming up from Wales.' I smiled at Mr Jeffries and turned to my aunt. 'Oh sorry,' she gushed. 'I didn't know you were in conversation. You must think me very rude.'

Having known Phyllis for over forty years, that particular aspect of her personality was never in doubt but I murmured a soothing disclaimer before turning around, hoping to pick up the threads of my previous tête-à-tête, albeit in a three way fashion. Unfortunately I was too late. Tommy Jeffries had gone.

CHAPTER III

I was suddenly alone for the first time in my life. I saw that clearly on the Monday after the funeral. Peter wouldn't be coming in half drunk at 6.30 every night. There would no longer be the sound of ricocheting bullets coming from the TV as he watched his beloved westerns.

All weekend I'd made plans for going back to work – maybe just part-time – just a little office job somewhere to earn enough to pay the rent and keep the fridge stocked – but the phone call I received on Monday morning made all that rather pointless. Peter's firm would be paying out £100,000 as he'd died in service – and it occurred to me immediately that his personal life insurance cover was of an equal amount. In short, I would never have to work again. I could live a life of leisure. I was 'comfortably off'.

I noticed the cigarette packet was still sitting on the coffee table. I hadn't given them a thought since I'd lit up on the day of Peter's death but seeing them there made me realise that I'd have to go through his 'things' and sort them out. I started with the cigarettes and threw them in the bin before I walked upstairs and entered his room.

It was the smallest bedroom in the house – but the small rooms they built in the 50s are bigger than some of the large rooms in the Legoland world of contemporary house building.

There was a TV and video – which I'd given him. They had originally been in my room, but he was spending so much time there – sprawled out on the bed – watching John Wayne and Jimmy Stewart that I decided he'd be better off having them to himself. I rarely watched anything on TV; I preferred the written word. There was a single bed of course; a small chest of drawers; a Queen Anne type chair and a writing bureau. My father had bought the bureau in the 60s. It had two drawers in it and a shelf at the bottom with sliding glass doors which acted as a bookcase. A built in cupboard held his stock of suits, shirts and ties. So, apart from a small music centre, there you have it. It seemed little enough to have amassed after fifty years on the planet.

I went into the cupboard and found an empty cardboard box, then I started with the books that were lined up in the bottom of the bureau. They were mostly detective or horror novels – although one that did catch my eye was a 'teach yourself' German book. I decided I would have to be brutal and put them all in the box which I'd placed in the middle of the floor. The bureau drawers contained only video tapes in which I had no interest so these were also packed into the box – which was filling rapidly.

I now turned my attention to the chest of drawers by the window. It invoked fond memories of how as a boy of fourteen I had opened the middle drawer one day while searching for a pencil to write up some school work.

I found more than I had bargained for. There before my very eyes was the latest edition of Penthouse. It's memories such as this that live with one down the years – the initial skip of the heart and the increased pulse rate which followed as I feverishly flicked through the pages with trembling hands. Francesca, Christianne, Penny – no one should underestimate the torment an adolescent boy goes through but the Penthouse was one of the highs of that time. God knows there were enough lows. Every teenager knows the horrors of Hell all too well – especially fat, red haired ones, of which I was a prime example. For about a year afterwards I'd checked in the drawer once a week or so – but there was never a repeat performance. It was just one of those wonderful things.

The box was always there though. It was a small wooden box with hand painted flowers on it. They weren't painted very well – in fact it all looked rather tacky. The padlock was too big for such a small box. I often wondered what could be in it and even picked it up occasionally to give it a gentle shake during my year of searching for Pet of the Month, but whatever was in it didn't rattle – it just made a slight noise to signify that the box wasn't entirely empty.

Even now I opened the middle drawer first and such is the power of the Pavlovian response that I felt my pulse rate increase – even after all those years. The contents were the same as always. No Penthouse – only the box – still there – exactly the same – same flowers, same padlock – it seemed rather bizarre in some ways. Twenty-eight years and nothing had changed. I picked it up and gave it a shake. The same sound assailed my ears. I lifted it out and put it to one side.

The other drawers contained various odds and ends; cigarette coupons; two unopened packets of Gaulois; a file with his life insurance policy in it, another with his credit card statements showing he owed £3,216.42p. That was a bit of a shock. There were some pens, pencils, a pocket calculator, two miniatures of whisky and an unused Filofax. Again the thought struck me that it seemed little enough to tell of a life. I emptied everything (bar the insurance policy and credit card paperwork) into the cardboard box which I had decided could go the local church's 'nearly new' shop. Surely someone would smoke the Gaulois?

The wooden box still lay unopened on the bed. There had been no sign of a key anywhere. Well, there was nothing else for it – I'd just have to use force. I walked out to the garden shed and got hold of an old hammer and chisel – it wasn't as if the box was a valuable antique or anything like that – its loss would not be a cause for concern during the conversation in the staff canteen at Sotheby's.

I had planned to hack away at the padlock but the hinges at the back seemed to be the easier option. I placed the box on the floor and held it steady with my feet as I hammered the chisel home. The success of my strategy was beyond my wildest expectations as the hinges flew off immediately and the lid flew up and struck my shin.

'Bastard!'

In my haste to rub my leg I compounded the problem by dropping the hammer on my foot.

'Bastard!!'

Why bastard? Why do we say that particular word. Ninety-five per cent of the male population of Britain would say 'Bastard!' in the same circumstances. I simply mention it as an interesting aside.

Having established that no lasting damage had been done to my person (by doing a Masonic impersonation and rolling up my trouser leg), I finally turned my attention to the contents of the box. Even before I picked it out I could see it was a photograph – one of those old sepia ones – brown and nostalgic. I could also see that there were two people in it, walking along the street, deep in conversation.

The brain makes snap decisions; I'd decided that it must be a photograph of my grandfather – though why it should be under lock and key in this box was not immediately obvious to me. That's what was going through my mind as I bent down to pick it up. I noticed there was a folded up piece of paper underneath it but I was concentrating on the photograph for the moment.

I know a frown appeared on my face when it came into focus – a puzzled frown – because I thought I recognised one of the men. The reason I was puzzled was that it didn't make any sense at all for his photograph to be in the box – after all, he wasn't family! It was an early photograph of him – before his frizzy, white-haired genius period – but it was quite definitely a photograph of Albert Einstein.

I gave a mental shrug of the shoulders, unsure of the implications of this discovery, and turned my attention to the man he was talking to. I think I actually blacked out for a moment – I know my pulse raced faster than if I'd found ten 'live' Pets of the Month standing in front of me. The fact is I was no longer simply puzzled – I was absolutely staggered – for Albert Einstein was walking along the street deep in conversation with my brother!

CHAPTER IV

Life is full of strange conundrums – we all know that – but what I was looking at wasn't a conundrum; it wasn't an enigma; it was a downright impossibility! It was something that simply couldn't be!

My head began to fill the illogical void with a view that this was one of those 'patched up' pictures such as one finds in the press, with the Prime Minister's head on top of a rock star's body. They're so realistic in this computer age that it's hard to see the join, but this explanation did nothing to erase the 'does not compute' message I was getting from the photograph itself. It was real – as I looked at it there was no doubt about it. It had an 'old' feel to it – there were no cracks or creases – it just reeked of its time.

What was its time? That was the next question which sprang into my mind. I put the 'impossibility factor' onto the back boiler and turned the picture over. In the movies there's always an inscription on the back – Paris 1926 – and the guy with the square jaw rubs his chin and looks thoughtful. I just sighed; there was nothing. I took it into my own room and examined it under a magnifying glass. There was no doubt about who the principal characters were. There were some people a little way behind them and a horse and cart on the road. It had to be fairly early in the century. I laughed out loud at myself for thinking this and looked at Peter again in an attempt to ascertain his age. He was young – maybe only 20 or 21. About the age he was when I was sneaking a read at his girlie mag!

None of it made any sense. I'd lived with Peter since the day and hour I was born. If he'd have met Einstein then I'd have known about it! What the hell was I talking about? Einstein died in – (I reached for my Factfinder) – 1955! Peter was five years old! Einstein was seventy-five! I slammed the book shut and threw it on the floor. Facts were no bloody use here.

I looked closely at Einstein in the photograph; he had black hair and a black moustache – he looked about twenty-five. When would that date it to? I picked up the book again and looked for the year of his birth. It was 1879. So that would mean the photograph was taken round about 1905. I quickly read through the brief biography. Einstein worked at the Patents Office in Berne from 1902 to 1908. Now that I studied it closely the picture looked Swiss – it had looked Swiss all along: if you had asked me at the outset to guess what country this photograph was taken in – I'd have answered 'Switzerland' immediately. The background had a definite feel of cuckoo clocks and neutrality.

I caught myself thinking that things were beginning to fall into place. Nothing could have been further from the truth. The whole concept was insane.

I suddenly remembered there was something else in the box! I had been so taken aback by the photograph, I'd forgotten all about the piece of paper. I went into Peter's room and grabbed at it eagerly; surely all would be revealed. The bizarre practical joke would be explained. It was folded in four and was an old, browned piece of headed notepaper Capital & Counties Bank, 221–224 Duchess Street, Glasgow. The writing underneath was a scrawl of black ink in a hurried copperplate style but after a few minutes study I was able to decipher it. 'Received from Mr Peter Bryson – one package to be placed in safe custody until called for.' There were two signatures; one – the clerk's – I couldn't make out, but the other was only too familiar to me. It read quite clearly 'Peter Bryson' and was dated '28/8/05'.

CHAPTER V

I didn't get much sleep that night. I'd started to make dinner for two at six o'clock and found myself in tears as I scraped what would have been Peter's omelette into the bin. The contents of the box wouldn't leave me; they harried me at every turn with their nonsensical, 'what came first, the chicken or the egg?' questions.

I looked at the photograph again and again. I think I half expected that I'd been hallucinating – each time I picked it up I thought it would have changed; that it would no longer be Peter – or at least not his younger self. But it was always Peter who looked out at me; his head half turned towards Einstein, his mouth open in speech; his hands held out in front of him – emphasising his point. Einstein was thoughtful; contemplative.

And where did my brother get a 1905 suit? I'd watched enough Edwardian dramas to see that it was a 1905 suit he was wearing – fob watch and all. I'd been through all his clothes that day, discarding some and packing others for the charity shops, but there was nothing remotely like that old suit among them.

Maybe I was making a mountain out of a molehill. Perhaps it really was my grandfather – family resemblance can be very strong – but I dismissed this even before I remembered that it was Peter's signature on the paper. There was no way of getting around it. I would just have to face the impossible head on.

That was reason enough for a restless night. I awoke tired and listless next morning but I was determined to follow up the bank lead. After all, I had an address and Glasgow was only a short train ride away. Having washed and shaved I made some bacon sandwiches and flicked through an old A–

Z street guide of Glasgow as I munched on my breakfast. Duchess Street was conspicuous by its absence. I had no reason to believe that the Capital and Counties Bank was still in existence either; ninety-five years had passed – things change. The one thing in my favour was that Glasgow was still there! That – and the fact that I still had some friends in banking circles who would be only too pleased to do some detective work for me. I phoned up Janice.

'Good morning, Commercial Bank of Scotland Coatbridge Branch, Janice speaking, how can I help you?'

'Cut the crap, Janice – I need a favour.'

'Excuse me?!'

'It's John, Janice – remember? John Bryson?'

Oh JOHN! How are you? It's great to hear your voice.'

'Just don't try to sell me anything.'

'I'll tell you – it's got ten times worse since you left. They'll be putting us on the game soon to get sales.'

'Then you'll be top of the pie chart.'

'Aw – that's nice – I think! Listen, I'm sorry about your brother.'

'Thanks Janice – I got your card. Ah well, at least it was quick and relatively painless.'

'That's true, but he was still young.'

'Yes – yes he was – but it comes to us all, remember it was your mother a couple of years ago and she was only sixty-two. Anyway, I'm looking to see if you can do something for me.'

'Certainly sir. We're here to provide a quick, efficient, quality service. Your wish is my pain in the arse.'

'Have you heard of a bank called the Capital and Counties?'

'No,' she replied slowly. 'Nothing springs immediately to mind. Are they a big outfit?'

'I've no idea,' I said. 'All I know is that they had a branch in Duchess Street in Glasgow in 1905.'

'1905!'

'1905.'

'Where's Duchess Street?' she asked.

'Damned if I know.'

'Christ, you are a typical customer – you know nothing. Wait a minute and I'll look up the book.'

'Thanks.'

She disappeared for a spell and then I heard the sound of pages being flicked over. The receiver was picked up again.

'John?'

'Yes?' I could see her smiling.

'What's this information worth?'

'A note to head office saying Janice Strang is helpful, friendly, patient, efficient and I'm so happy I'm a customer in the branch where she works. Will that do?'

'That would be lovely,' she laughed.

'So what have you found out?'

'Well – it appears that the Capital and Counties was taken over in the 1950s by one of our main rivals.'

'Namely?'

'The General Equitable.'

'What a wonderful woman you are.'

'You can put that in your note to head office as well.'

'I most certainly shall. One other thing.'

'Uh-huh?'

'Could you give me the phone number of the General Equitable branch in Glasgow?'

'I have my finger on it even as we speak.'

'I'm not interested in your sex life.'

'John! Behave yourself – there are quite a few branches actually. Have you any preference?'

'Yes – but just give me the phone number.'

She laughed. 'There's a branch in Argyle Street – will that do?'

'That's great.'

'0141 264 9851.'

'Janice ...'

'What?'

'If they ever put you on the game in there – make sure I'm your first appointment.'

'Get lost!' she laughed.

'I'll be in touch.'

'You should be so lucky!'

'Take care.'

'You too – bye.'

CHAPTER VI

I picked up the phone again immediately and dialled the General Equitable. An adenoidal young girl went through the usual introductory spiel. I allowed her to catch her breath before asking her if she could tell me what became of the safe custody items held in the Duchess Street branch of the Capital and Counties. My question had the expected effect – insofar as she said nothing at all for some considerable time – (presumably as she wrote it all down) – before giving a curt, 'Hold the line please,' and allowing me the dubious pleasure of hearing Mozart's Eine Kleine Nachmusik being performed on a digital synthesiser.

Time passed and having got over my initial shock I was now humming along with the mellifluous 'strings' when they suddenly vanished and the girl's voice could be heard in the background; 'Is it Eric?' she was saying. 'Old baldy Eric in customer accounts? Right – what's his number – does anybody know? Eric! What? Oh – right. Hello? Hello?' I held the receiver away from my ear as she bellowed down the line.

'Yes, I'm still here.'

'I'm putting you through to Eric in Customer Accounts – hold the line please. Thank you … is it 2438 you said?' Mozart reappeared briefly before a plummy voice took over.

'Good morning, Eric speaking. How can I help you?'

In an ideal world the girl would have passed my requirements onto Eric but this had obviously not happened so I repeated what I was looking for.

'Ah yes, sir – I remember it well. The old Duchess Street branch. I started my career there in 1954.'

'You must have started young,' I said.

'Fifteen, sir – yes, a callow youth of fifteen.'

'You'll have seen some changes since then.'

Eric sighed. 'I have indeed, sir – and very few of them for the better – if you don't mind me saying so.'

'I believe the Duchess Street branch closed at the time of the takeover.'

'Yes – that was in 1958 – it was a sad day. The Capital and Counties was my idea of what a bank should be, Mr Bryson; disciplined, secure, reliable. Every customer was known by name – every customer.' He sighed again. 'A different world.'

'Yes – the girl who put me through to you –'

'They can't even do joined up writing!' said an angst ridden Eric. 'They can't add – they need calculators to perform the simplest tasks.' He was almost in tears.

'You can't beat the good old days, Eric,' I said hastily.

'Indeed you cannot, sir.'

'You must be near retiring surely?'

'This year, Mr Bryson – four months to go – and it can't come quickly enough, I can assure you.'

'Quite right, you've done your bit for the cause – get out and let them all get on with it.'

'Just so, sir. Now, you were enquiring about the safe custody items from the Duchess Street branch.'

'Yes,' I said.

'Well, I can tell you from first-hand experience that they were taken to the Sauchiehall Street branch of the General Equitable.'

'First-hand experience?'

'Yes sir – I helped load the van myself.'

'Well there's a coincidence.'

'If you hold on I'll get the number for you – ah, here it is,' He read it out to me. 'And if you ask to speak to James Robertson I'm sure he'll be only too pleased to help you. James and I are old friends.'

'Well Eric, I can honestly say it's been a pleasure speaking to you. Thanks for all your help – and enjoy your retirement.'

'Thank you, sir. I'm very pleased you called. I'll spend the rest of the day reminiscing about my time at Duchess Street. Goodbye, Mr Bryson.'

'Goodbye, Eric – and thanks again.'

CHAPTER VII

It had just gone half past eleven when the train pulled into Glasgow Central. I had spoken to James Robertson over the phone and he'd told me if I brought in the safe custody receipt he'd see what he could do – '... But it was rather a long time ago,' he added as a get out clause.

I walked into one of the station cafes, ordered up a cappuccino and watched the world go by. You're probably wondering why I was wasting time when I was potentially so close to getting to the bottom of things. The problem was I was afraid I might find something in the vault I didn't want to know about.

I brought out the piece of paper from my inside pocket – the photograph was inside it. I still couldn't look at that image and make any sort of connection. The written words on the receipt were solid and sensible: Received from Mr

Peter Bryson – one package. There was nothing unusual there. Thousands of people put packages in safe custody – the only difference here was that Peter had managed to do it forty-five years before he was born!

Having decided to take Elvis's advice, in as much as it was now or never – I finished off my coffee and made my way through the lunch hour crowds to Sauchiehall Street.

The clerk at the enquiries desk led me into a side room and sent for Mr Robertson. It wasn't long before he arrived.

'Mr Bryson,' he said heartily, shaking my hand. 'Pleased to meet you.' I winced under his firm grip. 'Do you have the safe custody paperwork with you?' I took it from my pocket and handed it to him. He pursed his lips into a thin line 'Hmmm.'

He must have been near retirement age – like Eric. His straggly grey hair was shouting 'Hurray!' as if he'd been in a wind tunnel just before our meeting. He was definitely an eccentric character.

'This is a strange one, eh?' he murmured, taking a deep breath as he continued to scan the receipt. 'And you say you found this among your brother's personal belongings after his death?'

He was more like a doctor than a bank clerk. I was half expecting him to bring a stethoscope from his pocket and ask me to say 'ninety-nine'.

'Yes,' I replied.

He rubbed his chin with his left hand. 'Mmmm.' Suddenly his eyes met mine. 'It may take a little time to locate this item.'

I was somewhat startled by his piercing blue eyes.

'How long do you mean? Hours? Days?'

'Oh no,' he laughed. 'I certainly don't mean days – nor even hours – but we've reached the stage where the public deem twenty minutes to be an eternity.'

'I was taught that patience is a virtue,' I replied. 'Time won't be a problem.'

'So you're prepared to wait?'

'Certainly, if you don't mind.'

His face creased into a large smile. 'Capital,' he said rising from his chair. 'I'll be as quick as I can.'

As he disappeared out the door I felt that I was witnessing the end of an era. The extinction of a race of men and women who said things like 'capital'. It was a sad feeling – like seeing someone shoot the last dodo.

It was half an hour before he returned – his clothes liberally coated in dust and an ancient brown paper parcel in his hands.

'I do apologise for keeping you, Mr Bryson.'

'No trouble at all.'

'But the public perception of safe custody facilities is one of four walls of little stainless steel boxes full of stolen krugerrands and the likes.'

'I've seen the movies,' I laughed.

'Just so: the truth is somewhat more prosaic. Well,' he said, placing the parcel on the desk. 'I actually spent more time locating the paperwork than the package. Now sir, all that remains for me to do is to trouble you for some suitable means of identification – preferably in the name of John Andrew Bryson.'

He smiled at his joke, but his words stopped me in my tracks.

'How do you know my middle name?' I asked.

'Well, it's here on the parcel.' He turned it round towards me, 'And it's also on the paperwork. Can you see? It says 'To be collected by John Andrew Bryson'.'

CHAPTER VIII

I poured myself a drink when I got home. It wasn't something I was guilty of – drinking at home in the afternoon – but my nerves were frayed and it seemed to be a better idea than buying twenty cigarettes.

There had been no problem as regards identification. I had my passport with me and it quite clearly showed my middle name alongside a photograph which, in true passport style, looked nothing like me.

James Robertson had no hesitation in handing me the ninety-five-year-old parcel as if it was the most natural thing in the world. As far as he was concerned all the relevant criteria had been met. The paperwork stated that John Andrew Bryson would collect the parcel and John Andrew Bryson had duly collected it. The fact that John Andrew Bryson hadn't been born when the paperwork was prepared was neither here nor there.

I hadn't opened it yet. It was sitting on the table in front of me as I sipped at my scotch. I'd gone so far as to bring a pair of scissors from the kitchen to cut the string around it. It wasn't a hard parcel – it was soft; it felt rather like a pillow.

I leaned over, picked it from the table and sat it in my lap. One snip of the scissors was enough. With the string off, I unfolded the thick, crinkly brown paper and there it was – the suit Peter was wearing in the photograph. The photograph showed it in a sepia tint, but it was a good deal lighter in real life, almost light grey. I lifted up the jacket and felt in the pockets. Something was there – an envelope!

It was a long, cream envelope and it was addressed: 'Private and confidential. For the attention of Mary Morrison'. Whoever Mary Morrison had been she wouldn't be too bothered now about someone reading her private mail. I tore it open – only to reveal another envelope – with the same message: 'Private and confidential. For the attention of Mary Morrison'. There was also a single sheet of paper. I felt dizzy, drugged – I don't know what. It read as follows:

> Dear John,
> Sorry to be writing you a 'Dear John' letter – especially as I'm dead! Shame on you for opening someone's confidential correspondence! I'd love to say that everything will become clear in the fullness of time – but there's every possibility that it won't! Please keep the letter for Mary in the jacket pocket. There's so much I don't understand – so forgive me if I don't offer any explanations. Only Mary and Tommy Jeffries can be trusted – both for different reasons. Life is strange; remember nothing is ever

created or destroyed – nothing! Perhaps that's the strangest thing of all.

Your loving brother,
Peter

My brother had never written to me in his life. This was the only letter of his I had ever seen. As I poured myself another whisky I found myself trembling. My entire life appeared to me as being one giant misconception; I knew nothing about anything or anyone. My confidence and self belief lay in tatters around me.

The whisky burned my throat as I swigged it down. I knew it wasn't the answer – don't we all – but it's an escape of some sort – from one Hell to another. But is that what I wanted to do – escape? No! There had to be some rational answers to what was happening to me. I believed not in God, ghosts or vampires. Mankind had to stand on his own two feet and take responsibility for its actions – not grovel in the dirt and lacerate itself to invisible deities.

I shoved the envelope marked for Mary back in the pocket of the jacket. The suit trousers slid off my knee as I did this and there was a little bump as they hit the floor. I picked them up and stuffed my hands into the pockets. There was something in the right hand side. I knew what it was before I saw it – it was a fob watch. I could feel the cold metal in my hands as it emerged to face the light of day for the first time in almost a century, but it was only in that light of day that I noticed the wave-like ridges that encircled the copper coloured case. It took me a minute or two to collect my thoughts as it dawned upon me by degrees that the entire case had been soldered shut and was clearly never meant to be opened again.

CHAPTER IX

Of course I had to try the suit on. It ironed up beautifully and looked surprisingly modern. I could have walked outside without any sense of nonconformity. A ninety-five-year-old suit – and it looked as if I'd just bought it off the peg at C&A. The material was a bit rougher than its modern counterpart – a little courser – but if anything it was actually an improvement on its 21st century counterpart. It showed care and attention to detail in the way it was cut and put together.

I put the fob watch into the waistcoat pocket and fed the chain through a buttonhole. Looking in the mirror, I clutched the lapels like a high society lawyer and admired the way the watch chain glinted. No wonder suits never went out of fashion; they were impossible to improve upon – even the button-up fly was back in vogue. I pulled out the watch and was ready to open it and catch a glance of myself posing with it in the mirror (at least I'm honest!) but it was stuck fast with the solder. No problem – there was a soldering iron in the kitchen drawer. I'd bought it when I was in the Electronics Club at school and I hadn't touched it since 1974, but what the hell – a soldering iron doesn't change its spots; it would still do the job.

I managed to burn myself quite badly on the index finger of my left hand before I'd even started on the watch – but that was only to be expected given my track record in DIY. I was also foolish enough to hold the watch as I attempted to melt the solder surrounding it – I've no excuse at all, I know metal is an excellent conductor of heat – so that was another burn, on my palm this time.

It was twenty minutes before the last globule dropped into the empty ice cream carton I was using to catch the solder. Unfortunately the carton, being plastic, had melted in places and the solder had landed on the table. For a moment my head was filled with pictures of sandpaper and wood stain. These were but fleeting images however which I soon managed to shake myself free of as I ran my thumb along the centre rim of the watch and felt it click open.

There aren't any words to describe what happened next. I'll just have to write down the bare bones, as anything else is pointless.

I was somewhere else. It was a room with an old fashioned brass bed and an antique dressing table with a large mirror. In my amazement, I clicked the watch shut and was immediately back in my own room.

Do you see what I mean? How can I hope to put such an experience into words? Do you think you could do any better?

I simply sat down on the edge of the bed – so calmly, as to be comatose! I was there for a while, just rubbing the watch with my thumb as it lay in the palm of my hand. I knew I had lost my senses, yet I had no interest in trying to find them again! Finally I stood up and once again slowly moved my thumbnail towards the opening mechanism.

No sooner had I clicked it than I was back in the strange room once more. I frantically snapped the watch shut and lay down on my own bed.

It was an 'unexplained phenomenon'. That much was obvious. I certainly couldn't explain it. It would take a roomful of science fiction writers and nuclear physicists to work out what was happening. And yet I know that we take so much for granted: the fact that light travels at 186,000 miles per second; the fact that the earth hurtles through space at 67,000 miles per hour; the fact that the sun which gives us a tan is 93 million miles away; the fact that nuclear fusion between particles we can't see can destroy an entire city in Japan. These are the scientific facts we take for granted – but each of them is a phenomenon in itself. Think what it is to be alive; move your index finger up and down and try and explain how you're doing it: try and prove to a friend that two and two makes four.

The watch wasn't gold; it wasn't elegant or impressive. It was a solid, cheap Victorian watch – but wait – what was this? There was a cover on both sides. I'd been so taken aback by the front cover that I'd missed the fact that the back cover opened as well. To be honest, I was in no great rush to see what it revealed.

First of all, I stood up. If I was going to that other room again I didn't want to end up falling on the floor! When I'd plucked up enough courage I shut my eyes for a second and clicked the back cover open quickly. When I opened them

I was still at home – which was alright by me. I looked at the watch and came face to face with what I can only describe as some kind of small computer screen, but not the usual LCD screen we associate with computer technology. There was an iridescent background to this, changing constantly from red to orange to yellow – in fact going through the whole spectrum – all the colours of the rainbow in turn. There were no dials or buttons or anything like that, but the message on the screen was clear among the kaleidoscope of colour. It was in large, bold, black italic capitals and read – 1905.

CHAPTER X

I can hear you saying how I should have phoned NASA or the FBI, or gone to Roswell and tried to get in contact with the aliens who had created this technological miracle – but I decided to keep it to myself for the moment. It actually sounds rather silly if you say it out loud: 'I have a watch that can take me back in time.' Try it.

Call it speculation – but I was assuming that the room with the brass bed and old dressing table was from the year 1905. I once read one of those popular scientific books which appear now and then. It was all about black holes and contracting universes where broken coffee cups join together again and people get younger instead of older. It's the type of thing you pick up to pass a couple of semi-intellectual hours, rather than read the latest horror bestseller. I like to come away with something concrete from a book; that's why my mind's full of useless information – great for pub quizzes, but not much else.

So here I was, actually stuck in the middle of a 'science faction' book where the author writes: 'Imagine you were able to travel back in time – but of course then you could kill your grandmother and you would never be born – so how would you grow up to travel back in time?' This was me they were talking about. I had the technology in my grasp – literally – but for all I knew, my brother had already disposed of my grandmother several decades earlier.

I clicked the watch open again and the scene changed instantaneously. I'd love to describe how I fell through long, kaleidoscopic spiral tunnels – but that's not what happened. I was simply somewhere else, with no feeling of change to my person whatsoever.

'Peter, be a dear and pass me down my hatbox please.'

I almost died! So did she when I spun round on my heels. Her hand flew up to her mouth and she gave an involuntary gasp as our startled eyes met.

'Who – who are you?' she whispered, fearful and trembling.

I almost said, 'I don't know!' That's how much of a state I was in. It's one thing to find yourself in a strange room in another time, but it's quite another to discover there's a real person living in it!

'My name is John,' I blurted out at last. 'John Bryson.'

Her face assumed a puzzled expression. It was a very beautiful face – pale, with porcelain like skin; she was like one of those Victorian dolls that you see in antique shows on TV, with her hair tied behind in a bun: her eyes were soft, like a fawn's – big and brown – questioning.

'Are you Peter's brother?' she asked with a quizzical slant of her head.

'Yes,' I replied. 'I am.'

'But where has he gone? Why, he was here not ten minutes ago. We are going to see… Excuse me, Mr Bryson, but that looks very much like Peter's suit. Do you share the same tailor?

'Yes,' I replied through clenched teeth, desperately playing for time. 'Yes indeed we do.' I took a wild stab in the dark, 'Miss Morrison.'

'You know of me then?' she said quietly.

I tried to think what an Arthur Conan Doyle or H.G. Wells character would have said.

'Oh yes Miss Morrison. Peter has spoken of you on several occasions.'

She lowered her eyes and blushed – quite beautifully. The crafty old fox! I'd been here less than two minutes and had already discovered that Peter had – if not a girlfriend – then certainly an 'admiring acquaintance' in the shape of Mary Morrison.

'My brother has been called away on some urgent business and has asked me to accompany you to – your rendezvous.'

She gave a slight pout. 'He has not spoken of this to me.'

I gave as graceful a smile as I could muster.

'I assure you, Miss Morrison, both the suddenness and

the urgency of the matter that requires his immediate attention must be very singular indeed – as he informed me only yesterday that wild horses would not detain him from keeping his appointment with you upon the morrow.'

I wondered if I was laying it on too thick, but her eyebrows lowered again and a coy smile appeared on her lips.

'Your brother is a flatterer of some distinction.'

'On the contrary,' I interrupted. 'Having met you at last I can now fully appreciate his fervent desire to keep the appointment at all costs.'

'And you sir have obviously taken lessons at the same school of flattery. But come, hand me my hatbox and we shall be on our way for the hour of our assignation draws near.'

Two minutes later we were out in the street – and I was an extra on the set of an Edwardian drama.

The most incredible scents imaginable assailed my nostrils. There was horseshit, coal smoke, sulphur and sewage. Mary Morrison seemed to be completely unaffected by it all but I had never known my sense of smell to be put to such a test. The stimulus was a great joy – and, at the same time, an abomination. No wonder cholera and other diseases were rife; there was a stench of death and decay in the air.

'Wouldn't you agree, Mr Bryson?'

I hadn't heard a word she'd said: that was another thing – the noise – the sound of horses' hooves and people shouting: street vendors selling flowers, matches and God knows what; beggars and barefoot urchins running around screaming; a man with a hurdy gurdy and a little capuchin monkey.

'I'm sorry – you must excuse me, Miss Morrison. I did not hear your last remark.'

'I was saying the weather is fine for the time of year.'

'It is indeed,' I concurred.

'One so often associates April with showers – but I have kept a note of the annual weather cycle in my diary for several years and have found April to be my no means a month of rain – wind, yes – but seldom rain.'

'You astound me, madam. I would have thought April one of the wettest months of the year.'

'I can assure you, Mr Bryson, that the very opposite is the case. In my experience April is one of the driest months.'

'And the cruellest,' I said without a thought.

'Cruellest?'

'But that is neither here nor there,' I said hastily, cursing myself for my own stupidity – and Eliot for writing such a thing twenty years later! Mary Morrison gave me a look of some concern and we continued on our way for two or three minutes before she stopped outside a little tea shop and waited for me to open the door. As I stepped in behind her it was a shock to discover that she was making a beeline for a corner table – at which Tommy Jeffries was sitting.

'Mr Bryson,' he said affably, rising to meet me and shake my hand. 'We meet again.'

'I didn't know what to do for the best,' said Mary in anything like an Edwardian manner.

'You've done very well, Mary – very well indeed,' said Tommy patting her on the shoulder. 'The question is – what are we going to do now he's here?'

I was at my usual loss for words.

'This will doubtless have come as a shock to you, John – I hope you don't mind me calling you John,' said Tommy Jeffries.

'No, not at all – it is my name after all.'

'The thing is you see.' He put his index finger to the side of his nose and leaned over towards me, 'We're going to need that watch.'

'I don't understand,' I began.

'Of course you don't,' he laughed. 'How could you?'

Mary eyed Tommy nervously. 'Perhaps – we could – tell him,' she said haltingly.

'What good's that going to do?' said Tommy with his head cocked to one side. He was almost apologetic.

'I don't know,' she replied. 'I just think it might help.'

Tommy turned back to me. 'And would it?'

'Would what?'

'Would it help you? Knowing the full story? Do you think it would make it easier for you to understand all this?'

He waved his hand expansively, but there was no sarcasm in his voice. It was a genuine question.

'It might,' I answered quietly.

The two exchanged glances – then Tommy smiled.

'Let's have some tea then,' he said.

CHAPTER XI

Tommy bit fiercely into an Eccles cake and began his story.

'Mary and I come from what you would term – the future,' he said, rather indistinctly.

'The future?' I replied. 'How far in the future?'

'If you were from the future and an Egyptian stonemason was sitting here …'

'I see,' I said quietly.

'Now – even if you took one of your laptop computers back to the 18th century – no one would understand it. So to take it back to a pyramid builder would be…'

'And that's the state of affairs between the timepiece and myself?'

'Correct,' said Tommy with a broad grin. 'I'll tell you what though – there's nothing like these cakes where we come from – eh, Mary?' He sighed deeply. 'To think of what we had.'

'I don't know that I like the sound of that,' I said sharply.

He looked at me, and his eyes were filled with sadness.

'Deep down,' he said, 'you know. Mankind has always known.'

'So the future isn't any great shakes then?'

'The future's what you make it,' said Mary, breaking in angrily. 'There's an infinity of different futures.'

'Should you be telling me this?'

'Not really,' Tommy replied laconically. 'But Mary's the last of the future romantics.'

'I'm glad to hear that someone still believes in romance

in the future,' I said looking across the table at Mary. 'Oh by the way – I've got a letter for you.'

'A letter?'

'Yes, from Peter,' I said, drawing it from my pocket and handing it to her.

'Ooh la la,' laughed Tommy. 'A billet-doux unless I'm sadly mistaken. Aren't you going to open it then?'

'I'll open it in my own good time,' blushed Mary, shoving it into her small bag.

'I shouldn't tease her really – after all, it was my fault to begin with,' said Tommy.

'How's that?' I asked.

'I lost the watch the last time I visited; dropped it somewhere in London. They weren't best pleased I can tell you.'

Who weren't?'

'The Organisers.'

'Organisers?'

'You see, when you go on holiday you go to Greece or Spain, don't you?'

'Most people do – yes.'

'Well, when we go on holiday we go to whatever year we fancy – but we're not supposed to leave any equipment behind.'

'How did you get back if you lost the watch?'

'How would you get back from Greece if you missed your plane?'

'There's always another one.'

'Exactly.'

'I see.'

'We didn't think any more of the matter – until the watch was suddenly re-activated in 1974.'

'Peter went to visit Uncle George in London in 1974.'

'Yes, we know all about it; that's when he found the watch.'

'What – after seventy years?'

'It's amazing what you can find if you're in the right place at the right time. Look at Sutton Hoo!'

'Why didn't you take the watch off him? Why wait till now?'

'Peter became awkward – he started going on trips that we knew nothing about.'

'To Berne?' I suggested.

'You know more than we thought,' said Tommy.

'He wasn't doing any harm,' said Mary.

'WASN'T DOING ANY HARM!' shouted Tommy, who then lowered his voice as a few heads turned at the next table. 'Oh no – he was only altering the future.'

'My brother altered the future?' I gasped.

'It's no big deal,' said Mary. 'Let's face it, we all do it every minute of our lives – and remember, as I said before, there are an infinite number of futures. Tommy tends to forget that. But we really do need to take the watch back – for our own sake more than yours.'

'Then how am I going to get back to my own time?'

'Oh we'll take care of that,' said Tommy as I detached the watch and chain from my waistcoat and handed it over. 'It's just like taking the bus instead of the train.'

I looked across at Mary and she blessed me with a wonderful smile – and then, as I blinked, I was back home.

CHAPTER XII

I hadn't lost any time at all. It was as if I hadn't moved from the bed. The only thing I had to convince me that it wasn't all a dream was the suit.

I sat for about fifteen minutes then got up and changed into my own clothes. I knew that I wouldn't be able to throw the suit out – it held too many memories for me – so I packed it carefully in an old suitcase and put it in the attic.

It had just gone six and I realised that I was hungry. Cooking wasn't much fun any more – but I'd have to eat something. I stuck a beef curry in the microwave and started to fill the kettle. Then I heard the front door slam shut.

'Bloody points failure at Rutherglen. I've been sitting on that damn train for an hour. What's the bloody point of taking flexi-time, eh? Is that a curry? Thank goodness for something. Never mind about the tea – pour us out a beer, John – I'm going up to get changed.'

With that my brother bounded up the stairs as I stood with the kettle in my hand. The ding! of the microwave brought me back to my senses just as he came back downstairs.

'I'm going for the bus in future,' he said as he opened the oven. 'Hey, what's the SP here? This is for one!'

'I've already had something,' I stammered.

'Couldn't wait, eh? I don't bloody blame you. You'd be down to four stone if you were depending on me getting in on time at night with the state those trains are in. It's a bloody disgrace. Someone should do something about it.'

'It doesn't take an Einstein to see that,' I said quietly, sipping my beer.

His fork stopped in mid-air for a moment and for the merest flicker of a second his eyes met mine.

'No,' he said through a mouthful of curry. 'No, I don't suppose it does.'

CATHY

I

CATHERINE BELL was sixteen years old when she died. If she told me that once she told me a hundred times. She seemed to take some kind of perverse pride in the fact – as if she were aiming for a stick-out-the-tongue – 'I've done something you haven't done', effect. And she was right of course; I was – and indeed still am – very much alive.

I'll have to take you back twenty-eight years if you want to hear the full story. Of course there's no great necessity for you to turn the page. If you've read enough already by all means put me back on the shelf – but that doesn't mean the story won't be told – It'll still be there, within the covers, whether you read it or not; rather like Katie herself in fact.

'Don't call me Katie!' Yes – I can still hear her petulant little voice, even after all these years, and the passing of all those years has revealed to me just how true some of her – what I considered at the time – ridiculous utterances – have turned out to be. I'm thinking of one she was particularly enamoured of, 'You'll turn old and grey and wrinkly – but I'll always be sixteen'. That statement struck me with considerable force only this morning as I stared at my middle aged visage in the mirror.

AL PRESS

, SHERBORNE, DORSET DT9 4BS

T: 01935 814113

M: 07787 167972

info@sundialpress.co.uk

www.sundialpress.co.uk

of Distinctive Fiction

Date dispatched: Monday, 27 November 2017

THS OF TIME by David McGowan not
ou have a little time to spare. Twilight
n lightly upon the mundane, sometimes

LEWHITE

UK INDEPENDENT PUBLISHERS GUILD

THE SUN

SUNDIAL HOUSE, THE SHEEPL

SUNDIAL
MODERN CLASSICS
SUPERNATURAL
CONTEMPORARY FICTION

Publishers & Rep

Mark Andresen
25 Davies Avenue
Paignton
Devon TQ4 7AN

Dear Mark,

I enclose a complimentary copy of THE
necessarily for review but to dip into wh
tales in which the supernatural impinges
with a dash of mischievous humour.

With every good wish,

Frank

FRANK

THE SUNDIAL PRESS IS A MEMBER O

But don't start running away with the idea that Katie – sorry, Cathy – was a child prodigy in the philosophical field; nothing could be further from the truth – but then, what is the truth? That in itself is perhaps the most difficult question we ever have to answer. All I can do is give you my version of it and let you make of it what you will.

I was sixteen years old myself in the summer of 1975. It's a difficult age – sixteen. Much more so than eighteen or twenty-one; and the pressures on someone of that age are even more intolerable today than they were in my own time of 'hormonization'!

I had just left school at the end of May, having secured an O-grade in Metalwork and developed an abiding hatred of a certain Mr Leith, who taught Physics with all the cunning and vindictiveness of a vicious, belligerent child.

The summer of 1975 was one of the few during my time on earth which have actually lived up to their name. I can well recall passing out through the mid-Victorian iron school gates for the last time, literally jumping for joy at my new found freedom as only a man released from prison having served five years for a crime he didn't commit will understand.

My whole future lay before me; but that is the adult I have since become speaking – at that time I had no future before me, save the future of the next glorious hour spent walking through the fields, exulting in my great good fortune and savouring every second of a time I thought would never come.

At last I turned my steps homeward – mainly owing to

the fact that having eaten nothing for three hours I suddenly realised that I was absolutely ravenous. I had no watch – no way of knowing what the time might be – and yet even as I opened my front door I could smell the sausages that were sizzling under the grill and hear the hiss of the chip pan.

So there I was with school – as Alice Cooper had noted three years earlier, 'out forever'. Sadly Alice didn't think to inform us about what happens next.

'I've got you a start in Docherty's – but it's not till August,' said my father as we sat around the dining room table.

I must have visibly blanched, as my mother quickly volunteered an explanation.

'It's not on the shop floor – it's in the office – beside your uncle Dan.'

If this information was meant to console me then it signally failed.

'Didn't you say you wanted office work?' said my father – continuing before I had a chance to reply, 'You'll be alright – Dan'll look out for you.'

The fact that Uncle Dan had a glass eye imparted a surrealistic quality to this last statement – but I had no thoughts at the time of the one eyed man being king in the country of the blind; my thoughts were racing upon an entirely different course.

I couldn't argue with my father regarding his query about me requesting office work, as I recalled some months previously being asked if I'd take it if it came up. At the time I replied with a mumbled, 'S'pose so,' in much the same manner as if he'd enquired if I'd take joining the armed forces, becoming a train driver, being a private detective or the most illustrious explorer of my era! In truth I found it impossible to believe that my incoherent response that day could in any way be connected to my father's pronouncement at dinner.

'What was the date again?' my mother asked.

'The fifteenth.'

'Aren't you excited, Tom? You'll be a working man!'

I was very much excited – but not in the sense my mother was hoping for. Remonstrations of any kind however were completely useless. My father had spoken and his brother had pulled the necessary strings to get me in. What could I do?

You might say that it was my life and I should have stood up for whatever rights a sixteen-year-old had in 1975 – but that would merely show your ignorance of how things stood at the time. Fathers were figures who were obeyed in those days – or at least mine certainly was. To have raised any objections would have been to question his authority – and that was something that simply didn't happen.

Did I hate my father you ask? Why, no – I loved him; I loved him dearly and held him in the highest regard. It must be difficult for today's sixteen-year-olds to understand the conundrum here, but I can extrapolate no further and will have to leave it at that. I gave myself up to Fate, consoled by the fact that the 15th of August was still some six weeks away. At least I would have the majority of those glorious summer days to fill as I would.

My mind had wandered during this reverie concerning the six glorious weeks and I had obviously missed the thrust of my mother's most recent comment.

'So what do you think of that?' she said, addressing me across the table.

I had some vague notion that the last word she had uttered before this was 'tomorrow'. Being unwilling to admit to the fact that I hadn't been listening to a word she said I stuck half a sausage in my mouth with a noncommittal grunt.

'I told you he'd be pleased!' she beamed to my father. 'Didn't I tell you?'

'And so he should be,' came my father's sage reply, 'the fresh air will do him a power of good.'

Alarm bells began ringing in my head. I was obviously expected to go somewhere the next day. A sudden stroke of genius occurred to me.

'What time is it tomorrow?' I asked nonchalantly.

'Mr Chisholm didn't say a time – but I think you'd best go early – show you're keen. What do you think, Sam?'

My father nodded. 'Early right enough,' he concurred. 'There's a lot of work to get through there in six weeks.'

The clue was in the name of course. Mr Chisholm was the minister of the church my mother attended 'religiously' every Sunday. The information I had received did little to comfort me.

'Shall I go at nine then?' I asked confidently.

'Nine'll do nicely,' my mother replied.

I stabbed at a chip and transferred it to my mouth.

Another brain wave was required to get to the bottom of this mystery – and thankfully one presented itself to me.

'Do you really think it'll take six weeks?'

'Why yes – if you're on your own,' said my father. 'The grass is about two feet high – and I don't think old Chisholm will have much time to help you.'

At last I knew what my role was to be – cutting the grass in front of the church. But no, that couldn't be right. Mr Fredericks did that – and he did it so often that you could have played bowls on it. My chewing slowed and I lost my appetite as an image of the only place where the grass could conceivably be two feet high appeared before me.

'The graveyard!' I exclaimed.

'What about the graveyard?' My father asked. 'You're not scared, are you?'

'The way the question was formed ensured a positive reply.

'Scared? Who, me?'

'It's not as if you'll be there when all the ghosts come out at night,' my dad grinned.

'No,' said my mother. 'I told Mr Chisholm you wouldn't be there after six.'

'Six!'

'There's a lot of work to be done,' said my father. 'You'll have to take a scythe to that grass before you can think of using a mower – and there's a lot of places round those fallen stones where you'll have to cut the grass my hand.'

My mother nudged me with her elbow. 'You'll be

bringing in some money at last,' she smirked. 'Everyone ready for apple crumble?'

II

'It really is very good of you to volunteer young man. I'm sorry the remuneration is so low, but you know what church funds are.'

Mr Chisholm gave a gurning grin and a bead of perspiration on his bald pate began its slow journey down the side of his face. It was a gloriously warm day.

'Mr Fredericks has obtained the use of a scythe for us – and he's sharpened it to a considerable degree, so we must be careful, Tom.'

I wondered at his use of the plural here, as I had still to grasp the conception of the Royal 'we'. For a moment I thought that as there was only one scythe we would have to take half hour turns each with it – but only for a moment.

He led me round to the back of the church where I was able to see the task that lay before me. Six weeks? Hercules' cleaning of the Aegean stables would have been child's play compared to what my eyes surveyed at that moment. This was surely the largest graveyard in Western Europe. It stretched out like maize fields in the American Mid-West – an endless vista of long grass and weeds, swaying gently in the summer breeze. I turned my head to speak, but Mr Chisholm beat me to it.

'I'm sure you'll have it looking shipshape and Bristol

fashion in no time,' he smiled, handing me a long wooden shaft with a lethal looking blade attached to the end of it. I must have looked like Old Father Time when he was a boy as I stood there with the deadly device in my hand watching Mr Chisholm as he wandered back to the vestry.

As he disappeared from view I found myself with no other option but to make a start. But where to start? That was the question. I looked at the scythe then looked at the grass and finally swung the blade round – and thus my starting point was found. The grass dropped all around me and I saw how close I was to becoming a wooden-legged man as the weight of the blade carried it rather too close to my person for comfort. I swung again – a bit more carefully this time. Mr Fredericks had certainly to be applauded for his sharpening abilities. Again and again I swung the blade, gaining in confidence with each swipe. The swish of the scythe, and the hiss as it became the nemesis of all in its path, formed a steady rhythm for the next two hours – until I realised I was absolutely famished.

My mother had furnished me with a sizeable package containing six cheese and ham sandwiches, four chocolate digestives, an apple and a bottle of Irn Bru – so I had no worries on the score of going hungry and I was able to sit on the grass which I had newly cut and enjoy my lunch in the summer sun. The grass was not yet level of course – the scythe could not impart to it the bowling green shortness that Mr Chisholm required – I had to flatten it down a bit where I sat and surveyed my progress so far, munching all the while on some excellent Edam.

And I had made some progress – but even with the optimism of youth on my side I could see that making any real inroads into this jungle would take a very considerable time.

Still, that was what I had plenty of, and day by day as I swiped and swayed my way through the rain forest that was the churchyard I saw at last the truth of the old axiom that 'little and often will get the job done'.

It was during my third week that I first noticed Cathy. The previous day had seen me put the scythe down at last, the long grass having all bowed low to its majestic presence. To be perfectly honest I was sick of the sight of its curved blade and the blisters I had on my hands from its rough wooden pole were only then beginning to turn into the hard skin that constant work will bring.

I was in amongst the gravestones; there was nothing of the ghoulish about it – it was another beautiful day and I had always had a love of graveyards. It was the peace and quiet that appealed to me; the battle was over for everyone there and at last they could take their rest away from the everyday feverish madness that we call life.

As I said – I was tidying up the grass around one of the many gravestones. I had a pair of shears in my hands and they were clucking away like an old hen as I chopped at the weeds and stalks growing up around it when I suddenly became aware of a young girl who was sitting on one of the benches which were, at that time of day – it was late afternoon – in the shade of the perimeter wall.

I couldn't really see her very well, what with the wall

shading her and her being so far away – but the very fact of her being there struck me as being rather strange – unless she was some relation of Mr Chisholm's. This was the explanation my mind quickly settled on – and it soon became a thing of little or no consequence, as the next time I looked up from my task in hand she was nowhere to be seen.

It was three days later – a Friday afternoon – before I chanced to see her again. She was sitting in the same spot, but this time my diligent hard work had brought me that much closer to her and the grass I was shearing was only some thirty yards from where she sat.

She was a very beautiful girl – at sixteen that's the first thing I noticed – and I suppose that's the first thing men notice about the female sex no matter what age they might be. Her auburn hair hung in curls around her neck. She was wearing a rather odd looking outfit – a blue and white striped all-in-one skirt and top that seemed to button up the front – but what did I know about fashion! It suited her all the same – I remember thinking that – it hugged her figure and brought out her curves. Ah me – the trials of being a sixteen-year-old boy! She had a pale complexion and rosy cheeks – an unusual combination. I couldn't see the colour of her eyes from that distance but it didn't matter – I had already fallen in love with her.

'Tom!' I turned around at old Chisholm's shout. 'Your mother wants you to pick up some teabags from the shop on your way home.'

I nodded my understanding, and when my eyes turned

once more to the wooden bench it was only to see that she had gone.

III

It was a remarkable summer. Each day dawned in a glorious warm haze. Perhaps Constable captured that sultry laziness I'm thinking of best of all. Rain? What was that?

I continued to work steadily at my allotted task.

'You're doing a fine job, Tom,' said old Chisholm one day as he watched me trim the grass around the headstones. 'Yes, a fine job.'

I mumbled an appreciation of his comments.

'Another fortnight should see it completed, don't you think?' Again I mumbled as only a sixteen-year-old can. 'Splendid work Tom – perhaps you'll be kind enough to wood stain and varnish those benches at the back – if I can get Mr Fredericks to provide the materials.'

Needless to say the next week found me stripped to the waist with a pot of wood stain and a brush in my hand. Thankfully Fredericks had done the sanding himself, so all I had to do was apply the stain and – when that had dried – the varnish.

When I had finished I picked up the cans and took them over to the back door of the church, pausing only to turn around briefly to survey my handiwork from a distance.

The shock I received was not only from seeing her sitting there – I was really more concerned that her dress would now be ruined and I cursed myself inwardly for not putting up a 'Wet Varnish' sign the minute I had finished. With an audible sigh I dumped the tins I was carrying and began running over the grass to make her acquaintance and warn her of her folly of sitting in the midday sun.

When she wasn't there I knew all was not as it should be. She had only been out of my sight for a couple of seconds as I dumped the tins; barely time for her to rise, never mind walk out of view – or even climb over the wall.

As I reached the bench she had been sitting on my sense of unease heightened measurably. The varnish was still shining in all its sticky glory in the summer sun and it was certain that no one had been sitting there at all.

I sat down on the grass and tried to make some sense of what had just happened. I've never put much faith in a sixth sense but all at once I had an uncanny feeling that someone was standing behind me. I turned my head to find she was some six feet away, looking at me as if I was an exhibit in a glass case in the Natural History Museum. I noted – with some satisfaction – that she at least had the decency to blush under my own interrogating gaze.

For a moment we remained silent, eyeing each other up – not in any man/woman way, or not in my case anyhow – it seemed more like a boxer assessing his opponent.

'What's your name?' she asked abruptly.

Her voice was not what I expected it to be; it was somehow 'different' from any I had heard before. Many people had faced me and said exactly the same words, but none had uttered them in such a genuinely interested questioning tone. It probably sounds nonsensical, I know.

'Tom,' I replied.

Her brows furrowed slightly and a moment later another question formed on her full pink lips.

'Do you live here?'

'No,' I laughed. 'What, in the manse do you mean? No. I'm only working here.'

'Working?' She seemed confused.

'Yes, working – cutting the grass, varnishing the benches, things like that – just helping out Mr Chisholm.'

I could see her confusion deepen and for a moment I thought it was going to get the better of her. A great internal struggle flashed across her features; her mouth opened as if she was about to speak, but then the placid young girl returned and she smiled – as if at her own self.

'What's your name?' I asked.

'Catherine,' she replied, kicking the grass bashfully.

'Are you from around here?'

'I'm from over there,' she said, pointing to the far wall.

'What – Glebe Street?'

'No,' she giggled, 'over there.' She seemed to be pointing to the wall itself. 'Come, I'll show you,' she said, gaily taking me by the hand and leading me at a trot through the tombstones. I noticed she had a crescent shaped birthmark on the back of her right wrist, the vermilion showing up prominently against the background of her pale skin.

It was only a matter of seconds, but it was the first time a girl had ever held my hand. It should have seemed forward of her, but her innocence enabled her to carry it off without the slightest hint of anything sexual – even I could see that, for all my raging hormones.

'There!' she said, as we came to a sudden halt. She was smiling cheerfully and I can still remember how the sun shone through her auburn hair. When I looked down it was to find we were in front of a stone which bore the inscription:

Catherine Bell
1786–1803
Died aged 16 years

IV

'Tom! Tom!!'

That's my wife – Christine – shouting. 'I'm up in the attic.'

'Tom!'

'Up here!' I heard her footsteps as she started up the stairs.

'What are you doing up there?'

I popped my head through the attic entrance. 'Just tidying up a bit, seeing if there's anything we can give to the church jumble sale next week.'

'Well don't be all day – remember we're going to my mother's at three.'

'Whoopee doo,' I grimaced.

'I'm going down to the supermarket to pick her up a few things, but I'll only be an hour or so.'

'OK, I'll be organized by the time you get back.'

'Right – I'll see you later then – bye.'

'Bye, love.'

I went back to the photograph album I'd been looking at. Old Chisholm had wanted some pictures of the 'new look' graveyard for the church magazine that summer, and there I was – all those years ago – standing next to Cathy's gravestone. I'd love to report that she was there too – a ghostly apparition in the background – but that wasn't the case.

I'd made tentative enquiries at the time about church records etc. to see if I could find out any more about her – but it was too long ago; her life – and death – remained a mystery.

So much had happened in the past month of 2003, but my mind was on a more distant past.

V

Even as we stood hand in hand by the stone that summer, I felt her palm 'melt' in my own and I knew that ghosts did indeed exist. I asked her about this the next time we met.

'Where do you go to when you're not here?'

'Somewhere.'

'But where?'

'I really don't know.' Her brow furrowed slightly in concentration. 'It's rather like … do you know where you go when you dream?'

'No.'

'Well,' she beamed, 'it's just like that.'

'Do you remember me when you're there?'

'Sometimes I think I do – but I'm not terribly sure; you know how difficult dreams are. Do you remember me?'

'Of course I do! I'm alive!'

'Really? Then I must be dead I suppose.'

'But of course you are – you're buried over there!'

'Dead, dead, dead,' she intoned.

'What did you die of?'

'I've no idea – perhaps it was a disease.'

'Can't you remember dying?'

'It's all very well for you! You're still alive! It's very difficult to remember things when you're dead.'

'You must have been quite rich.'

'Rich? Why do you say that?'

'You speak very well, very … properly.'

'One's vocabulary obviously has no bearing on one's longevity!'

'Do you remember your parents?'

'No,' she replied simply.

'Aren't they there with you?'

'I don't believe so – I'm not really sure.'

'It must get very lonely if there's no one there.'

'Oh I'm sure there are people there – it's just that I can't recall who they are. But I don't think I'm lonely – besides, I've got you,' she smiled. 'Are you lonely?'

'Of course not – I've got my family and friends – and you.'

'But you remember them all of course.'

'Yes, I do.'

'That would appear to be the only difference then.'

'What?'

'The only difference between being alive and dead.'

'No it's not – there's loads of differences.'

'Such as?'

'Well – I can't just melt away like you for a start!'

'But I don't mean to!' she replied forcefully. 'I don't want to. It just happens.'

'But why?'

'I don't know.'

I reached for her arm. 'You're so solid!' A sudden thought struck me. 'Maybe you're from a parallel universe!'

Her blank expression brought it home to me that half the solar system was still waiting to be discovered by the time Cathy died – so the concept of a parallel universe was slightly out of her reach.

She looked into my eyes. She was so simple; so trusting; so beautiful. I saw then that she was as much in love with me as I was with her. It was the most wonderful moment in my life up to that point. She was still gazing at me as she faded. I never saw her again.

VI

Of course I pined – but who could I confide in? It was a ridiculous tale; I would have been put on medication if I'd ever mentioned it. The graveyard job completed, I joined the 9–5 mob at Docherty's for two years and then went into banking for the following twenty-five.

I met Christine in the bank and we had the obligatory two children and a house in the suburbs where we did the things that people in the suburbs do until Eleanor and Richard grew old enough to fly the nest and make a life of their own. They were gone within a year of each other, leaving Christine and I looking across the living room at each other wondering who this stranger was.

Did I love Christine? What a difficult question. Probably not – the only person I ever truly felt what I believe was love for had died two hundred years ago. I had never mentioned Catherine to Christine. I'm sure that won't come as a surprise!

I felt a shiver there – someone walking over my grave. I look so young and full of life in that photograph by Cathy's grave. It was taken the day after I'd last seen her and I fully expected her to return at any minute. But she never did. Maybe those others she felt vaguely aware of put the kybosh on her ramblings – I don't know.

I would never forget her. How could I? But life goes on, and mine did too as I described, and we all plodded along in true textbook fashion – until last week.

VII

Those Customer Service courses really piss me off. I'm forty-five years old now and I've no wish to go to some hotel in the middle of nowhere in England and listen to an acne-faced twenty-year-old whizz-kid tell me how the customer is the Number One priority in banking – when the real hidden agenda is, 'screw the bastards for every penny you can'.

But what could I do? It would be lovely to turn round and say, 'Shove your Customer Service course up your arse,' but my job would be shoved up there with it – and there's the mortgage to pay for a few years yet and the pension to think of as well.

I didn't have any choice. Three of us were picked to go on the course; Pete was twenty-two, Roberta was twenty-three – I was forty-five. They would have a great time getting drunk all night and going at it like rabbits – but all I wanted was to get to bed … to sleep.

It all went exactly as I thought. We arrived there at 7 p.m. and ordered up some dinner. The 'kids' were kind enough to put up with me without making it too obvious that they'd much rather be alone, and I for my part was decent enough to bolt down my meal and retire to my bedroom as quickly as possible so that they could get down to some serious drinking – and whatever else they had planned.

From their performance the next day it looked as if they had over indulged in pretty much everything. As a team we were crap. When my individual efforts were all that carried us through, I gave them notice at dinner that they'd better get their act together for the next and final day of the course. I've no doubt they both gave me the finger the minute my back was turned.

When it was turned I wandered into the bar and ordered up a scotch. When I'd finished it I ordered up another one then looked at my watch. It was 10.30 p.m. – time for bed. I threw the whisky down my throat and moved towards the exit – just in time to see the 'lovey-dovey' Pete and Roberta come in from the other side. They didn't see me, and that suited me fine.

I marched up the plushly carpeted stairway and made my way along the corridor to my room. There was a woman a few paces in front of me. The light was rather dim, but she seemed to be about my age. She stopped at the door two down from my own and her hand reached out to turn the handle.

I don't ever expect to have that feeling again – that feeling as I caught sight of the crescent-shaped birthmark on her wrist. I honestly thought my heart would burst from my chest.

Instinctively I reached for her hand on the door.

'Cathy!'

She gasped and her head whirled round. For a moment I saw fear in her eyes – then confusion. It was as if she knew I was right – but she didn't know why. That's when I kissed her. She offered up no resistance. As our lips parted her eyes met mine again – still questioning as she opened the door. I closed it behind us and gently cradled her face in my hands.

'Cathy.'

She kissed me this time and I began fumbling with her blouse. Her skirt fell of her own accord as I reached round to undo her bra. It fell to the floor amidst my shirt and trousers. She was truly beautiful. I cupped her breasts in my hands and marvelled at their softness. My thumbs caressed her nipples and she gave a gentle sigh and closed her eyes. My lips moved down to kiss her neck and then moved to those gorgeous globes and we fell back onto the bed.

Her soft, smooth, satiny skin enraptured me. Her scent was heady – like mystical mead – and my tongue experienced sensations it had never dreamed of as she sighed and moaned beneath me. I looked into her eyes as she guided me within and there and then I realised that the soul in no fiction, the soul is a fact – a fact beyond reality.

She held me tightly as her climax approached, but there were no wild cries of 'yes! Yes! YES!!!' The single tear that escaped her eye and trickled down her cheek was the catalyst of my own eruption – my own personal tidal wave of such exquisite intensity that I thought I should never survive it. What we shared had nothing to do with sex – that much I do know.

I grew soft still inside her. Her breasts were rising and falling with each short, sharp breath she took and I could feel both our hearts beating, wildly at first, then more sedately as we floated back down to earth from Nirvana. My head was leaning just over her right shoulder.

'I love you,' I whispered softly in her ear.

She made no answer, but I could feel her smile. It was the happiest moment of my life.

I must have fallen asleep – not the greatest surprise in the world, given the state I was in. I woke with a start and instinctively reached for her, but all my arm fell back on was the bedsheets – she had gone and once again I felt the loneliness of Yeats' 'Wandering Aengus'.

'Though I am old with wandering,
Through hollow lands and hilly lands,
I will find out where she has gone,
And kiss her lips and take her hand.'

I had long believed that Aengus died a lonely old man in pursuit of his glimmering girl, and I felt sure any search I undertook would run along similar lines. Women and men were made to torture each other, and as my tears wet the pillow I was in agonies that Torquemada himself could never have inflicted.

VIII

There was nothing in the room; her clothes were gone. Not a sign remained to say that she had ever been there.

The desk clerk swore the room was a vacant one – and I was left to ponder how she had managed it; how she had come back; how she had aged – just as I had – and how she had loved me all those years, just as I loved her, so that we knew each other without knowing each other – if that makes any sense.

'Tom! Are you STILL up there! Come on – we've my mother's to go to!'

I don't expect to see Cathy again in this world. I think it took every bit of her thirty years of guile to manage what she did. But I do believe she's smiling somewhere, in the midst of her shadowy protectors – smiling, and waiting – for I won't live forever.

CAT'S EYE

FELIX (original or what?) lost his right eye during an altercation with Tyson, an American pit bull terrier well noted for his grumpiness. As it was the Yank's third offence he was swiftly taken away by the authorities, anything but quietly it must be said, and within a few hours he had been despatched to the golden grandeur of the big pet cemetery in the sky. Weep ye not.

Felix's 'landlady' (for no cat ever had an owner), a mid-fifties spinster by the name of Gwen, nursed her charge back to health, albeit to the serious detriment of her bank balance, and within a month Felix was fit enough to resume his midnight prowls on the backstreets of his old stomping ground.

So far, so boring you may well be saying and, as things stand, I would be hard pressed to disagree with you. However the interesting fact of the matter is that although Felix had lost an eye, he had found another one, for somehow the 'plucking out' that had occurred opened up a pathway to his third eye; his inner eye.

'Mystical claptrap!' you say, but I would ask you not to close the book and put it in the charity shop bag just yet. At least permit me the opportunity to explain how I came to be involved with Felix in the first place.

My name, by the way, is Philip – though I'm better known as Phil. I met Gwen when I became a member of the local history society. As we were both unattached we drifted together, while making it mutually clear all the while that we were perfectly happy with our unattached status, though meeting for a coffee now and again seemed a not unreasonable idea. Gwen is an extreme 'tidy-upper'; the last thing she wants is a man leaving her toilet seat up – and the last thing I want is a woman who has a panic attack when she opens up a new bag of eighteen toilet rolls and, realizing it's her last one, hurries off to the supermarket forthwith.

When I first met Felix both his eyes were still firmly in place. He employed them to give me a cursory glance, decided I was of no consequence whatsoever and settled back down again in front of the fire. As for myself – I hate cats. For Gwen's sake I gave a forced smile and moved towards puss to give him a friendly pat. His eyes soon told me that any attempt at such familiarity would result in my instant death. I sat down and nervously nibbled a digestive while awaiting my coffee.

'Have you and Felix made friends?' asked Gwen bringing through the cups from the kitchen.

'Oh yes,' I lied. 'We're best mates.'

Felix lazily opened the eye he would soon be losing and fixed on me a look of such contempt I believe I blushed.

'He really is a little darling,' she gushed.

'I can see that,' I replied with a fixed grin. 'Is he a good mouser?'

'Oh no!' gasped Gwen in wide-eyed horror. 'I don't allow anything like that. Felix would never do anything like that.'

A hint of a Cheshire smile appeared on Felix's lips and I saw at once how things stood. It was the smile of a Caliph with a wife who is unaware of his harem.

I was on holiday in Sweden when I received Gwen's text about the spat with Tyson. Of course I was effusive in my condolences in my reply and then immediately forgot all about it. Indeed I viewed it with regret that Tyson hadn't torn the head off the supercilious feline. It was some six weeks later when I found myself once more at Gwen's place.

'And he's really made remarkable progress, all things considered,' she was saying as she led me through the hall.

'Well, he'll still have eight of his lives left,' I said cheerfully as she opened the living room door.

I noticed the change at once. He had aged in some way. Not that his black fur had turned grey overnight or anything like that – but there was something in his demeanour that spoke of 'elder statesman'. I was reminded of Charlton Heston playing Moses. Felix had matured. He'd had both youth and middle-age knocked out of him.

'He's still my little pussikins, aren't you Felix,' cooed Gwen tickling him under the chin. This was no way to treat Moses – and he showed his contempt, even with one eye – though there was no malice contained within it.

'And of course he likes you, Phil,' she went on. 'I'll go and make the coffee.'

Left alone I felt as nervous as a schoolboy being taught physics by Einstein. Felix obviously no longer actively despised me – I could see that much – but whether he liked me or not was a point on which I remained unclear. He approached me in a fearless fashion and sat down beside the chair in which I had parked myself.

'No sugar – is that right, Phil?' came Gwen's voice.

'Yes, that's right – milk only please,' I replied – just as I realized, he wants me to pick him up!

It seemed like an order, not a request and, bending down slowly, I complied with it. I was as stiff as a board. There was something in Felix's remaining eye that had never been there when he had two. Gwen was opening the door and bringing in the coffee when I heard the voice in my head.

'What exactly are your intentions towards Gwen, sir?'

'Well!' cried Gwen. 'He's in your lap! He doesn't even let me do that.' I was too busy trying to fathom out how a cat could both speak English and be telepathic. 'You're honoured indeed.'

'And you sir – are you going to honour me with a reply?'

Three way conversations are confusing at the best of times, and the odd slant of this one wasn't helping.

'My intentions are strictly honourable,' I said – or thought – or … whatever, impressed that we had all managed to fit 'honour' into our preceding sentences.

'Biscuit?' asked Gwen holding out a tea plate.

'Indeed sir? That's too bad – as I think she's quite taken with you.'

'Thanks,' I said grabbing a Hobnob.

'I'm going to dine now, but I'll be seeing more of you in the future.'

So saying Felix leapt from my lap and strode majestically to his food bowl. The funny side of his final statement was obviously lost on him.

II

He was, however, true to his word. In the days that followed he was forever making the short walk between Kirk Road and Glebe Street that separated my terraced house from Gwen's semi. His first visit found him in a philosophical mood.

'I've no idea what has happened to me, but I feel sure there must be a reason for it,' he said as I spread some marmalade on my breakfast toast.

'You believe in Fate then?' I replied. 'That everything is pre-ordained and we are merely marionettes dancing to a piper's tune over which we have no control? That it was in the universal scheme of things that Tyson should maul your eye out?'

'I think it must be – perhaps it was the only way to make contact with you.'

'I recall trying to make contact with you on our first meeting,' said I. 'The reception I received was – somewhat frosty shall we say.'

'I was a cat then,' said Felix tetchily.

'And you're not now?'

He thought for a moment. 'No,' he ruminated. 'I'm certainly no longer a cat.'

'Then what are you?' I asked presenting him with a saucer of milk.

'I'm a man in a cat's body.'

'Perhaps you'd prefer the toast then.'

'Look here,' he began angrily before suddenly breaking off and saying urgently, 'Come at once.'

'What? Where?'

'Gwen's.'

'Why on earth would I go to Gwen's at this time of the morning? It's only just gone eight.'

'Come!' he hissed. 'You must!'

Something in his manner affected me. I put on my coat and shoes and followed him out across the street.

'Don't ring the bell – there's no time. The door's open – go in.'

'I can't just go in!'

'You must!'

I went in. I could smell burning immediately. Pushing into the kitchen I found a cereal packet had fallen onto a hotplate that had been left on full power. 'Jesus!' Flicking the 'off' switch on the wall I filled a pot with cold water and poured it over the burning mass. The flames had reached the nearby kitchen roll, which I picked up smartly and threw into the sink – just as Gwen came rushing in wearing her pyjamas.

'Oh!' she gasped. For a moment we were both lost for words. 'I smelled burning. I put it out. It was the Corn Flakes. The kitchen roll was on fire too.'

'Oh my goodness! But how did you …?'

'I was just bringing Felix back. He had wandered over to my place. I was going to leave him outside your door when I …'

'What a gift from the gods you are,' she swooned. 'I would have simply panicked.'

'Not at all. I'm sure you –'

'Oh but I would have. The whole house would have gone up in flames while I dithered about what to do. I'm like that you see. I'm no good in a crisis.'

'It's hardly a crisis.'

'I can assure you it would have been – but for you.'

Her pupils were dilating as my stomach was sinking. 'Think nothing of it. You carry on with – whatever you were doing and I'll tidy up here.'

'Oh no! I wouldn't dream of it. You must let me tidy up the mess – you simply must! Please, take a seat in the front room. I'll just throw on some clothes.'

With that, and an arch look in my direction, she went upstairs.

'This little escapade hasn't done you any harm, Phil,' smirked Felix. 'No harm at all.'

I was in no mood for his shenanigans. 'How did you know?'

'It was in her eyes, old man. She's obviously –'

'I'm not talking about that – I'm talking about the fire!'

'No idea I'm afraid. I simply knew. Sixth sense and all that. Must come with the new territory. Has its uses though, what?'

'Could you please stop talking like a colonial major in an Agatha Christie book?' I pleaded.

'Sorry old boy, looks like I'm stuck with that too.' There was a pause before he started up again. 'She's well-heeled you know – owns this place. Got a tidy sum put by as well if I'm not mistaken. It'll all go to some damn fool niece in Cornwall if you don't –'

'Will you give it a bloody rest! I'm not interested!'

If a cat can shrug its shoulders then he did. 'Suit yourself.'

Despite Gwen's previous protestations I went into the kitchen and began to clean up the mess. It wasn't too bad, but I gave an involuntary shudder as I imagined how things could have turned out.

'Phil! You really must leave that to me,' said the fully dressed Gwen when she arrived a couple of minutes later.

'I'll just take all this out and put it in the bin,' I said, indicating a large roasting tray into which I had put the 'burnt offerings'. 'Unless you fancy toasted Corn Flakes for breakfast?'

She grimaced and let me pass as she stood in the doorway. We were almost touching and a flush came to her cheeks.

'I'll scrub the sink then make some coffee,' she said hastily. 'Please go and sit down when you come back in.'

I did – and began to play drums on the back of the chair with my fingers.

'Must you do that?' said Felix.

A thought struck me. 'I don't suppose you know this week's lottery numbers? Racing certainties? Football results?'

Felix's lips set in a grim line. 'Lowest common denominator, eh? You humans are so predictable.'

'Well aren't you one now?'

'Not in that way, I assure you. I don't know how my gift works, but I am secure in the knowledge that it wasn't given to me to tell you that Millwall are going to win three nil on Saturday.'

'Are they?' I asked seriously. He answered with a disdainful look. 'It seems to be the way of 'gifts',' I went on. 'They never appear to serve any useful purpose.'

'So you think saving Gwen's house, and probably Gwen herself, from being incinerated serves no useful purpose?'

'That's not what I mean.'

'Then what exactly do you mean?'

I sighed. 'I suppose it's just a pipe dream.'

'What is?'

'Millwall winning three nil – you seeing the Derby winner.'

Felix stretched on the carpet. 'I'll tell you what I can see though,' he said.

'What?' I asked. His eye closed. 'What?' I repeated. It opened and closed again. 'What are you doing?'

'I'm winking,' he replied.

'Winking? You can't wink with one eye!'

'I suppose the meaning might well be 'lost in translation' so to speak,' he agreed.

'Are you still going on about –?'

'Yorkie's today, Phil,' said Margaret with a huge smile, handing me a tea plate. 'Chunky,' she added, raising her eyebrows.

III

The following afternoon found Gwen and I sitting in a room in the library at our weekly history club meeting, listening to a talk on local ecclesiastical buildings which was being given by the retired Dr Terence Peterson. If I'd been asked to hazard a guess at his age I would have plumped for 136. His voice droned on in a seemingly never ending sepulchral monotone.

'St Mary's was first erected in 1782 …'

'He was probably a founder member,' I whispered to Gwen, 'and I'll bet that's the only erection he's seen in the last fifty years.'

She guffawed and covered it up with a loud cough as she slapped me on the knee. The people in our vicinity weren't impressed, but we were oblivious to their 'tuts' and carried on giggling like a couple of school kids. I was having fun. Gwen, prim, proper, matronly Gwen was having fun too. We were having fun together. It felt good. In fact it felt so good that when the interminable talk was finally over I asked her if she'd like to go out for dinner some night.

'You mean out out?' she asked.

'Is there an in out?'

'Like – a dinner date?'

'Gwen – we're both fifty-five – we've been around the block, I think we enjoy each other's company so why not?'

She nodded and that was that.

Felix was very pleased of course.

'Finally seeing sense, eh? Quite right, you shouldn't look a gift horse in the mouth.'

'It's got nothing to do with that. I'm financially independent.'

'All the same – can't have too much of a good thing, what?'

'We're going for dinner, Felix, not getting hitched.' He closed his eye. 'Are you winking?' I asked.

'No – concentrating. I can see you both walking down the aisle.'

'Are you having a laugh?'

'Yes,' he smiled.

Six months later we were married.

Other SUNDIAL SUPERNATURAL titles:

FROM ANOTHER WORLD
by ROSEMARY TIMPERLEY

THE ALABASTER HAND
by A.N.L.MUNBY

MIST And Other Ghost Stories
by RICHMAL CROMPTON

THE ROOM OPPOSITE
And Other Tales of Mystery and Imagination
by FLORA MAYOR

A PAD IN THE STRAW
by CHRISTOPHER WOODFORDE

GHOST GLEAMS
Tales of the Uncanny
by W.J. WINTLE